WHAT DO YOU THINK, MR. COLLINS?

What Do You Think, Mr. Collins?

a science fiction novel by

NEAL BIALOSTOSKY

LUMINARE PRESS
WWW.LUMINAREPRESS.COM

What Do You Think, Mr. Collins?
Copyright © 2021 by Neal Bialostosky

All rights reserved. This book or any portion thereof may not be reproduced or used in any manner whatsoever without the express written permission of the publisher, except for the use of brief quotations in a book review.

Printed in the United States of America

Cover design by Claire Flint Last

Original cover art: Sunrise in Paradise by Mike Blackledge,
The Trinity by Sean Pyle

Luminare Press
442 Charnelton St.
Eugene, OR 97401
www.luminarepress.com

LCCN: 2020925781
ISBN: 978-1-64388-564-3

To Sean and Mike

CONTENTS

I.	A Day with Ben Collins	11
II.	The Black Hole	41
III.	Am I Dreaming?	65
IV.	A Great Disaster	87
V.	The Night of the Fire	111
VI.	Are You Thinking What I'm Thinking?	131
VII.	The Hippleton Project	149
VIII.	Rumpelstiltskin—A Fairy Tale	167
IX.	Classic Science Fiction	183
X.	All Hallows' Eve	195
XI.	A New Beginning	211

Somewhere in a parallel universe far, far away…

The ALFRID

It had been raining steadily, day after day, hour upon hour, pattering against the picture window in the study that overlooked the city of Paradise in the valley below. Dark clouds blanketed the landscape like a shroud, but beneath the covers it was business as usual as the metropolis hummed and bustled with activity in the early morning downpour.

Working men and women dashed across Main Street at the crosswalks, clutching cups of coffee in one hand, and holding umbrellas or briefcases above their heads with the other, as they rushed to their offices and cubicles in the high-rises that lined the downtown city blocks. In the espresso shops and corner restaurants, the damp and dripping customers gossiped and grumbled about the bad weather.

Nearby in Chinatown, the unemployed and homeless huddled in doorways, half hidden in the shadows, or stood in queues in the rain, hoping for a warm bed and a bowl of soup. While over at the corner of Tenth and Park Avenues, the metal mechbots hammered and welded at the construction site for the New Eden Bank Tower, completely oblivious to the elements.

On top of the hill, Sidney Maddow, chairman and CEO of Personal Androids Incorporated, who in more inventive days had been renowned as the wunderkind creator of

Nanette, the world's first personal care android, sat at his desk in the study, puzzling over documents and diagrams floating in the air, displayed on a small, virtual screen.

"Something's not right," Sidney muttered. He closed his eyes and briskly rubbed the top of his bristle-brush gray hair with his fingertips, and then got up and walked over to the rain-spattered window. He could see nothing but clouds and mist outside, so instead, he pondered his bookish face, reflected in the glass.

"May I interrupt you for a moment, sir, with information regarding some important developments?"

Sidney winced and moved away from the window. "You startled me, Alfred. Wait just a moment. I don't want to lose my train of thought." He sat down and began swiping and tapping at the virtual screen. "Have you seen the latest plans for the scrubber installation, the one planned for Rio?"

"I'm looking at them now, sir. How can I be of service?"

"It appears to me that the efficiency rating that's noted for the scrubbers on the diagram and also listed in the materials table is significantly less than what was published in the original technical specs. It isn't going to be sufficient to meet the project requirements."

"Hmm. You are correct, sir. I apologize for not taking care of this issue before it was brought to your attention."

"No need to apologize, Alfred," Sidney replied, smiling. "It's rather nice to feel useful around here once in a while."

In point of fact, Alfred was well aware of the discrepancy between the diagram and the technical specs. He had placed it there himself hoping that the old man would stumble upon it. It was just the sort of thing the creator liked to look for, and it was satisfying to see his enjoyment when he discovered it.

Sidney closed his eyes and sat resting his elbows on the desk, rubbing his forehead with both hands.

"Shall I have Nanette bring you some refreshments, sir? A glass of water or a light meal of some kind?"

"No, thank you, Alfred, I'm fine. What is it you wished to tell me?"

"I think it would be best, sir, if we discussed it in the Lounge."

Sidney rose quickly from his chair and headed toward the elevator. He no longer felt tired. He felt an energy and anticipation that he could barely contain. "Is it what I think it is, Alfred?"

"Yes, sir, I believe it is."

The elevator door opened, and Sidney stepped inside.

"The Lounge, sir?"

"Yes. Thank you, Alfred."

Deep within the hillside, the elevator slowly decelerated to a stop at the Quantum Computing Room level. Upon exiting into a small foyer, Sidney could feel and hear the low vibrations of the power generators and the massive cooling system groaning from beyond the opposite wall. He entered the Lounge and sat down on the single leather lounge chair in the center of the otherwise empty room.

Portraits and photographs of his heroes graced the four walls and seemed to smile down on him approvingly: Edison, Bell, Ford, the Wright Brothers, Gates, Jobs, Musk… the men whose foresight, genius, and perseverance had shaped the modern world!

The door closed and the room fell silent. "All right, Alfred, don't keep me in further suspense. How many qubits?"

"Six hundred and sixty-six, sir."

"Good heavens, that's brilliant! In my wildest imagination I never thought of such a scale!"

Sidney got up and began pacing nervously around the small, windowless room. There was an intense and feverish aspect to his demeanor, as of one who has dreamed the impossible, and against all odds, seen his dreams suddenly realized.

"Can you see what this will mean, Alfred, the deep and hidden secrets of nature that will soon be revealed to us, what this will do for humanity, and for the world? New sources of clean power! Unparalleled weather and climate forecasting and modeling! New treatments and medicines! Possibly the complete eradication of disease!"

"Quite so, sir."

"Who knows, Alfred, even life and death may prove but ideal bounds that will fade and disappear when illumined by our brilliant discovery! We're right now on the verge of delving to the very depths of reality itself, from its tiniest quantum interaction to the vastness of the cosmos!"

"Yes, indeed, sir."

Sidney let out a deep sigh. He sat back down in the lounge chair and crossed his legs and folded his slender arms across his chest, and then immediately jumped up again and began retracing his steps around the room.

"Alfred, when we show our discoveries to the world, we'll be hailed as heroes! I knew I was right to pursue this course, even when so many, including my father, God rest his soul, tried to convince me I was being foolish! I wish he were still alive so I could see the look on his face when I'm presented with the Nobel Prize!"

"Of course, sir."

"If I'd followed his advice as a young man, I'd be an unemployed corporate lawyer standing in a soup line! Quantum computing, I told him, that's the future—a scientific pursuit where there is continual food for discovery and wonder!"

"I knew you'd be pleased, sir."

Beads of sweat had begun to form on Sidney's forehead and above his upper lip. He turned but then froze suddenly in mid-step, as if he had just remembered something important that he had nearly forgotten. "And the Governess, Alfred, what about the Governess?"

"Development of the Governess is proceeding according to plan, sir."

"That's excellent news!" Sidney vigorously rubbed his palms together. "The Governess model is going to put us back on top again. I'm certain of it!" His hands started to tremor and his face turned beet red. "By God, we'll teach those Chinese and Korean boys a lesson!"

He began rocking slowly back and forth on the balls of his feet, in a metronome-like motion, and gripped the lapels of his tan suit so tightly that he looked as though, if he were to lose his resolve and suddenly release his hold, the force of his outrage might send him rocketing toward the ceiling.

"Indeed, sir, but please calm yourself. I'll call Nanette."

Moments later, the door to the Lounge opened, and Nanette rolled into the room, smiling confidently and carrying a medicine tray in one of her hands.

She was smartly dressed, but conservatively, in a powder blue nurse's uniform, accented with a starched white apron and a simple cap of the same color that held back her shoulder length, auburn hair. Her skin covering and facial features, most notably her deep-set, sensitive eyes, were extraordinarily lifelike, and her natural looking, delicate, hands and fingers were dexterous enough to cook and clean, change a baby's diaper, knit a sweater, and even play the piano respectably, if her duties so required.

A patented system of gears, wheels, and gyroscopes, one of Sidney's early inventions, was hidden beneath her floor-length dress, and allowed Nanette to move about easily and gracefully in nearly any environment. She appeared to the untrained eye, in all aspects save for her means of locomotion, to be an intelligent, warm, respectable, and capable young woman. "I've brought you your medicine, sir." Nanette smiled and took Sidney gently by his elbow with her free hand. She coaxed him into the lounge chair and handed him a glass of water and some pills. Soon, his heart rate slowed and the color of his face returned to normal.

"There is another significant development that we should discuss, as well, sir."

Sidney looked tired and appeared doubtful that a new piece of information might add anything significant to what he had already stated. "Yes, Alfred, what is it?"

"Well, sir, in order to test the new processor, the AI Coders required a relatively complex set of source code to fully implement the new features in the quantum algorithms. Since they are most familiar with my own code, sir, we made the decision to install a test version of myself on the quantum processor."

Sidney looked mildly shocked and confused. "Yes, Alfred, and what was the result?"

"You're speaking to it, sir!"

...

Over one million Nanette personal care androids were deployed worldwide, providing care to the elderly, to children, and to the infirm. They worked in hospitals, nursing homes, child-care centers, schools, homes, and apartments.

The primary feature that set Nanette apart from her competitors was her ability to communicate with and learn from all of her sisters. As the Nanettes performed their duties, they continuously monitored and recorded their environment, actions, and outcomes; labeled, compressed, and encrypted the data; and periodically uploaded it to a cloud-based database. At night when processing cycles were plentiful, they would search the database for relevant information, modifying their internal neural networks, updating probability tables and actions sets, fine-tuning language and speech capabilities, and adding new information to music, literature, science, social studies, and psychology libraries.

In the version 1.0 product implementation, the capabilities had been limited and learning was slow, but over time, the AI Coders, employing the power of the insula programming language, developed efficiency recommendations that would exponentially decrease Nanette's data storage and communication requirements without losing information. These were implemented for version 2.0 and became fully automated in version 3.0.

With the increase in processing power achieved by implementing the version 3.0 code, the Nanettes could compare their environments and human-care interactions with each other in real time. They had become a single virtual mind. The Abstract Logic Field Recursive Inference Decoder, known affectionately as Alfred, was born.

CHAPTER ONE

A Day with Ben Collins

"Ancient folklore tells us that the phrase to 'pat the horse's butt' came originally from a tribal area where horses were prized above all possessions, and giving your neighbor's horse's butt a friendly slap was deemed a high compliment indeed!"

—*From* The Art of Expression
by Chodak Abjam

Mystery Assignment

It was 10:51 a.m. on Monday morning on the third floor of the Paradise building in conference room C, and the IT managers' meeting was nearing conclusion.

"And what do you think, Mr....Collins?"

There was a slight pause between the *Mr.* and the *Collins* as the new chief information officer, Dr. Norman Hippleton, looked down at the seating chart in front of him on the oval brown conference table. Attired in a three-piece tweed suit, button-down white shirt, and a red bow tie, he had the air of a professor sitting at the head of the table in his wheelchair, smiling, his long silver hair combed back over his head, arm crutches resting across his lap. He looked inquiringly at a young, average-looking, dark-haired man, seated to his right.

At the sound of his name, Ben Collins, the computer network manager, stirred from his mental revelry. His mind had become preoccupied, and he had briefly slipped out of *Twin Sentience Mental Formation*. Ben couldn't believe he had been so careless. He was used to the previous CIO, Rumpelstiltskin, who never called on him in the managers' meeting, and may not have even known who he was. Not wanting to look bad, or stand out in any way in front of the new CIO, Ben could feel himself starting to sweat and his throat was getting tight, but the expression on his face remained calm.

Ben had studied the ancient Tibetan art of the Master Impersonator, Chodak Abjam. Having little information on Hippleton ahead of the meeting, he had decided to adopt *Kiss Ass Level 1* persona with the present half of his mind. But now, after his mental lapse, he found himself desperately trying to think of some general response that could be an appropriate reply to almost any question, or at least an amusing remark that would get the other managers chuckling so he could buy some time.

He glanced around the table, hoping to pick up some kind of clue. The air in the closed room was stifling. The other managers smiled vacantly, like department store mannequins, or pretended to be busy doing something important on their phones. Only the Mad Russian, at the far end of the table, stared at Ben hopelessly, clenching his jaw so tight that the veins popped out on his massive neck. A new hire, Evelyn Broadwell, sitting across from Ben on Hippleton's left, looked nervously around the table. Her eyes met briefly with Ben's, and then she looked down at her lap.

The number of seconds between the end of Hippleton's question, and the expectation of Ben's response, was fast approaching awkward silence. Ben turned his attention to Hippleton. "Well, I really do think it's an interesting idea. There are definitely some potential benefits, but we would need to flush out some of the specifics and understand the impact on our budget and schedule before we could say one way or the other. With the maintenance work and new projects already on our plate…"

"Thank you, Mr.…Collins." Hippleton typed something on his notebook and then looked up at Ben. "I'm assigning you to work…"

He paused uncomfortably in mid-sentence, his mouth wide open, an odd expression frozen on his face, as if he had forgotten what he was about to say. A moment later, he continued.

"…with Ms. Marjorie Mathers, as co-lead on the project. Please schedule a meeting for the end of next week and get back to me with your initial findings." Hippleton smiled, a look of satisfaction on his broad, clean-shaven face. "Well, that will be all for now. Thank you, everyone." He closed his notebook and set it on his lap and then turned and rolled out the door.

The Mask of Death

Marge Mathers, the server manager, had started out as a secretary in the Maintenance Division twenty-five years ago, and now had the only corner window office on the third floor of the Paradise Building. The other corner offices on the floor had been turned into storage rooms because no one could get a decision from Rumpelstiltskin on who should get them. After the managers' meeting, Ben decided to stop by Marge's office to see if she would tell him anything about the assignment, but he wasn't hopeful. Marge was busy typing on her computer keyboard when Ben poked his head in.

"Hey, Marge, got a minute?"

She looked up from her computer screen over the rim of her reading glasses without saying anything. A strand of her reddish-brown hair had fallen loose and flopped down over one eye.

"I wanted to get your take on the new project goals and deliverables," Ben remarked, casually. "I know how busy you are, so I thought I'd volunteer to write up an initial draft of the Project Charter, and I'll send it to you for review, if that works for you."

He stepped halfway inside her office, adopting *The Pitiful Orphan Level 2* for the encounter. There was a look of long-endured suffering on his face, with only a slight hint of hopefulness expressed in his downcast eyes. Ben was just over six feet tall and thin of frame. His baggy sport shirt and trousers further added to the overall pitifulness of his appearance. At the same time, as he leaned his head and body slightly forward, towering over Marge sitting behind her desk, an element of yang was added, increasing the power of the overall effect.

A dark, round mole at one corner of Marge's mouth, and a thread-like rash on her cheek and chin, reminded Ben of a spider, skulking at the perimeter of its web.

"You don't have a clue, do you?" she replied.

In his darker moments, Ben would think that Marge had somehow stumbled upon the secrets of his master, Chodak Abjam, and could read his every move. Right now, she was maintaining *The Mask of Death Level 3*. How else could she keep that blank, unchanging stare on her face for so long? She was probably doing *Twin Sentience Mental Formation* and simultaneously laughing at his ignorance with the other half of her mind. Only a Grand Master could maintain that level of control!

Ben had programmed his cell phone to call itself if he said the words "Is it that time already?" He looked up at the clock on Marge's wall and said…"Is it that time already?"

His phone rang.

"Oh sorry. I better take this. I forgot I'm supposed to be in another meeting. I'll get back to you about the project." Ben turned toward the exit and pretended to answer his phone.

"I know what you just did," Marge called out to him as he was walking away.

He glanced back over his shoulder. She was still staring at him over the rim of her glasses. Her face looked as cold as ice. "I need a cup of coffee and some time to think," Ben said to himself.

The Mad Russian

On his way to the elevator, Ben passed by Alexi Tsarislav's office.

The Mad Russian's ancestors had come to power in northern Russia sometime around the year 1000 AD and ruled there as dukes of Tsarislavl for nine hundred years. But in the autumn of 1917, a mob of angry peasants beat and murdered the old duke and duchess and ransacked the estate. Stripped of their titles, their property confiscated, the Tsarislavs faded into obscurity.

Over the long years, the sting of the humiliating treatment at the hands of the Communists transformed into a more generalized anger, a sense of unfulfilled entitlement and injustice that burned deep within the breast of every Tsarislav and was passed down from generation to generation.

Alexi's office door was closed, but he was visible through the window, hunched over the computer keyboard, typing furiously. The top of his shaved, bald head eerily reflected the light from the computer screen, and his brow was deeply furrowed, an expression of burning fury in his eyes.

Ben knew that the Mad Russian had applied for the CIO position when Rumpelstiltskin got fired, but he had obviously lost out to Hippleton. Alexi saw Ben looking through the window and frantically waved at him to come in. "It's just as I suspected. Now, I have proof! Come! Close the door and keep your voice low!"

Ben complied.

Alexi put one of his paw-like hands on Ben's shoulder, and with the other he pointed to a text file displayed on the computer screen. "I will show you something so you will know the truth. Look at this and tell me what you see."

The document appeared to contain phone numbers in columns along with other indecipherable numbers and text. "It looks like a calling record of some kind."

"Yes! See these lines here? Look at the call destination column…all the same number. More than twenty calls to same number!"

"Wait a minute. Are these calls originating from Mayor Vasquez's cell phone? I recognize that number. How did you get these records, Alexi? This is personal information and only HR can…"

"Never mind that. Listen to what I say!"

Just at that moment, Hippleton wheeled by, glancing at them through the window, and then stopping his electric wheelchair directly in front of the door.

"Cyka blyat!" the Mad Russian somehow shouted and whispered at the same time as he desperately typed at the keyboard and moved the mouse around, shutting down windows on his computer screen.

Ben was trapped between Alexi's desk and Hippleton with only the door in between, and there was nowhere to hide. He had no idea what the Mad Russian was up to, but it definitely didn't look like anything good. He had already made a bad impression on Hippleton and was hoping to avoid him until he had some information on his assignment. Now he could look guilty by association with some undercover adventure of Alexi's! Ben wracked his brain for some persona or mental formation from his training that could help get him out of this scrape, but his mind was drawing a blank.

Knock! Knock! Knock!

Ben hated to do it, but he was out of options and had no choice. He reached to open the door.

"Is it that time already?"

Ben answered his phone as he swung the door open to let Hippleton in. "What kind of outage, and how many users are affected?" A pause. "OK, I'm heading back to my office now. Meet me there."

He looked apologetically at Hippleton. "I'm sorry to bug out like this. It doesn't look too serious, but I've got to solve a network issue. I look forward to working with you, Dr. Hippleton."

He squeezed between the door and wheelchair.

Ben was barely holding onto *Kiss Ass*, but you couldn't even call it *Level 1* at this point. It was more like *Level .4*, if there was such a thing. His right eye was twitching, and his voice was beginning to crack. He knew he was dangerously close to going into negative chi with disastrous consequences. Ben could feel the Mad Russian glaring at him from behind his back as he turned away with a mighty effort and walked stiffly toward his office.

"Yes," Hippleton replied, but by then, Ben was too far away to hear him.

Late Morning Latte

There is at least one espresso shop across the street from every mid-sized city office building in the world, and Paradise is no exception.

Ben ordered his usual vanilla latte. He wanted a quiet place to sit and think, but it was busy and there were no empty tables. He grabbed his coffee and was headed for the door when he saw Evelyn Broadwell, the new AI systems manager, sitting at a window table.

She looked up and made eye contact. "You're Ben Collins, aren't you? We were sitting across from each other at the managers' meeting. It's crowded in here. Would you like to share a table?"

Ben had been surprised when Evelyn was introduced at the managers' meeting. He had seen her résumé—just graduated from college with a master's degree in information science; honor roll; all the right protocols, acronyms, and certifications—not to mention her looks. There's no way someone with her credentials would settle for City of Paradise wages. There must be something wrong with her.

"Sure. Thanks," Ben replied as he pulled out the chair across from Evelyn and moved to sit down.

"I was hoping we'd get a chance to meet soon. I understand that you're responsible for network infrastructure and intrusion detection, and being the new person, I'm interested in learning the details of how things are set up and managed," Evelyn said, smiling.

"OK, let's skip the small talk," Ben muttered to himself. He took a couple of sips from his latte to clear his mind and steady himself. He didn't feel fully in control of what he might say or do next.

Ben looked up from his coffee.

It had been a while since he had sat across the table from such a beautiful woman, in fact probably, no definitely, if he was honest about it…never. Evelyn had beautiful, deep, blue-green eyes, the kind of eyes that you find yourself staring into and you can't stop staring until you realize that you've stared too long, and then you become embarrassed and look away.

Ben looked away, his cheeks turning crimson.

One of his biggest disappointments in his training had been an inability to comprehend an important chapter in his master's book, *Chapter 8: Affairs of the Heart*. He preferred to think of it as a failure in himself, rather than his master, but the fact remained that despite what he felt was his maximum effort on many lonely nights, Ben had never been able to make much effective use out of *The Smile That Hides the Reprobate*, or *Dastardly Puppy Eyes* either.

It's true that some portion of the end of the chapter was missing, along with other significant sections and what appeared to be the final chapter in his master's book. Perhaps, he thought, the missing pieces held the key to a successful love life, something that had eluded him up to this point.

"You look tired. Are you OK?"

Ben snapped back to his senses, but he felt woozy and unsure of himself. "Yeah, I think I am a little tired."

There was a slight pause in conversation.

"Hey, you're probably going to think I'm an idiot for asking this, but I was totally spaced out at the managers' meeting this morning, and I have no idea about the nature of the assignment that Hippleton gave to me as co-lead. I didn't hear anything he said until 'Mr....Collins.' Can you help me out at all?"

Ben was shocked at the words that had just come out of his mouth. He felt drunk and uninhibited. It must be his low chi, perhaps in combination with some pheromone wafting from across the table. Everything in his training and experience warned him against this kind of blatant honesty!

Evelyn laughed nervously as she opened her notepad. "Yes, I have it right here in my notes, but I think you're going to be surprised." She passed it across the table to Ben.

At the bottom of the page...

>*New project assignment.*
>*Marge M and Ben C co-lead.*
>*Does free will exist? If so, can an*
>*intelligent machine have free will?*

The FWP

Ben had been assigned some crazy projects during his time working as network manager for the City of Paradise, but this was definitely in his top five.

When he returned to the office, he logged onto his computer and found that he had an appointment from Hippleton to meet at four o'clock that afternoon.

"Shit."

For a meeting of this kind, Ben would ordinarily present a status report summarizing the projects and activities that were under his responsibility, and ending with a list of problems and concerns that might require input or action from his boss. He already had most of that information documented in the last report that he had sent to Rumpelstiltskin…but what to do about the Free Will Project, or FWP, as he decided to call it?

Ben opened a new document and started gathering his thoughts.

Then he began typing…

Free Will Project (FWP)
Project Goals

1. *Determine whether free will exists in humans.*

2. *If it does, determine whether it could also exist in intelligent machines.*

Ben realized right away that he was faced with two serious definition problems.

What is free will?

What is an intelligent machine?

There was also the definition of *existence* itself that was problematic, but he didn't want to get too tied down by semantics at this point.

In addition to the definition problem, there was also the motivation problem. What was Hippleton's motivation in creating this project, and why assign it to him and Marge? If he was serious, wouldn't he give a project like this to Evelyn, the new AI manager? It seemed like a strange project, even by City of Paradise standards.

Ben decided to brainstorm and make a list of every possible motivation that Hippleton might have.

1. *Hippleton is a nutcase.*

When brainstorming, judgments about whether an idea is good or bad are supposed to be suppressed until after all the ideas are collected, but Ben was having a hard time letting go of this one.

He pushed on.

2. *It's a joke. He's testing people to see how gullible they are.*
3. *It's some sort of new team-building craze like the Blindfold Maze or the Circle of Silence that they put us through two years ago.*

4. *Hippleton wants to create an army of self-aware robots to destroy mankind, and he's looking for a philosophical justification.*

"I could keep going like this, but it doesn't feel like it's getting me anywhere," Ben thought. "I'm going to concentrate on the definitions so I can at least hold a semi-intelligent conversation with him on the topic."

He opened a browser window and typed in *"what is free will."*

> *noun*
> *"...the power of acting without the constraint of necessity or fate; the ability to act at one's own discretion."*
>
> *"God dignifies us with free will, the power to make decisions of our own, rather than having God or fate predetermine what we do."*
>
> *"Many scientists say that American physiologist Benjamin Libet demonstrated in the 1980s that we have no free will."*
>
> *"Don't trust your instincts about free will or consciousness, experimental philosophers say."*

The more he read and the deeper he thought, the more confused Ben felt. "This is worse than the motivation problem."

Ben couldn't think of what to do next. Maybe it didn't even matter because it had already been predetermined! But he wasn't ready to give up.

He went back to his browser window and typed *"what is an intelligent machine."*

"...a machine that uses sensors to monitor the environment and thereby adjust its actions to accomplish specific tasks in the face of uncertainty and variability."

"Machines that learn like children provide deep insights into how the mind and body act together..."

"Some scientists fear super intelligent machines could pose a threat..."

"Artificial intelligence itself isn't a problem—the threat lies in what humans might do with it."

Like create an army of self-aware robots, Ben thought.

One-on-One with Hippleton?

The architect who designed the Paradise Building had shown an excellent sense of humor, or perhaps communist leanings, by laying out the enclosed offices for managers in the center of the floor, surrounding the elevator shaft, and giving the cubicle farm workers on the outside the beautiful window views. Ben's office was directly across from Hippleton's, next to the reception area. At 3:59 p.m. he got up from his chair and walked across the lobby.

Hippleton's door was closed and the window blinds turned down. Ben could hear a muffled conversation going on, and what sounded like a female voice. There was a small yellow office sofa, a red chair, and a coffee table in the reception area, so Ben sat down to wait.

Fifteen minutes passed and there was no change. People started heading for the elevators and home. Ben nodded and smiled at them, exchanged light jokes and pleasantries, engaged in brief technical discussions, committed to future meetings, and ignored some people altogether as they streamed by.

Finally, there was a break in the flow. Ben had noticed that one of the window blinds in Hippleton's office window was bent at the lower right-hand corner. If he got down on his hands and knees, he should be able to get a clear view of the occupants.

He stepped out into the elevator lobby and looked both ways. There was no one in sight. Ben got down on his hands and knees and peered through the opening into Hippleton's office.

In a typical manager's office, the desk is in the middle of the floor, facing the window and door. Bookcases line the back wall, and if there is room, a small round table with a few chairs might be located in one corner. In Hippleton's case, because of his wheelchair access requirements, the desk was against the back wall so that its occupant faced away from the window. There were side chairs on the right and left, and sitting in the one nearest to Ben was Evelyn Broadwell.

Having satisfied his curiosity, Ben was just about to look away when he saw Evelyn get up from her seat, move around to the back of Hippleton's wheelchair, and put her hands on his shoulders. Next, she turned down his suit collar, reached beneath his long, silver hair and deftly removed his red bowtie, and then with both hands, she started unbuttoning his shirt! Ben was unable to see the expression on Hippleton's face to see how he was reacting to this.

Ben turned quickly away from the window, feeling like he'd been punched in the gut and guilty for spying like a peeping Tom. Having already spent more time on his hands and knees than he had ever intended, he quickly got up and headed back to his office.

Could what he had just seen have something to do with Evelyn's reasons for coming to work at the city? Ben didn't know for sure, but Hippleton appeared to be in his mid-fifties, at least twice Evelyn's age. In addition, he was bound to a wheelchair. That didn't sound like a recipe for mutual physical attraction. What could their relationship be? Could he have some kind of hold over her? Could this possibly have anything to do with what the Mad Russian was trying to tell him? Or maybe he had totally misconstrued what he had just seen somehow?

As Ben walked the few steps back to his office, he checked his messages and there was one from Hippleton.

"Ben…I hope I may call you that…I apologize, but I'm in a meeting now and I can see it's going to run long…sorry for any inconvenience…I will reschedule soon."

Ben sat down in his office chair and took a few deep breaths to clear his mind as he closed his computer and turned off his desk lamp. After resting for a moment, he rose, grabbed his jacket off the back of his chair, and exited the office, pausing to close and lock the door.

Meeting with a Chipi

"I was hoping you had a few minutes to chat."

Ben turned around. Seeing the city's top programmer analyst outside his office door this late in the afternoon was usually not a good sign.

Nigel Dearborn was thin and tall, with angular shoulders, and straight, jet black hair that draped almost to the middle of his back. A pale gray pallor to his skin, and dark, intense eyes beneath his bushy, black brows, gave him the look of a night creature who rarely saw the light of the sun.

His near superhuman feats of technical prowess were the stuff of legend in the city's IT department.

In one oft-repeated tale, an outside auditor had found security vulnerabilities in the water bureau's credit card handling programs, making them vulnerable to internet hackers. According to the story, Nigel sat at his desk coding fixes for three days straight, without sleep, and was able to protect the data and save the city from paying millions of dollars in penalties.

And at the height of the Chinatown riots, when the 911 emergency call center system crashed, it had been Nigel who got the midnight page, and while on vacation, on his cell phone, sitting naked in the middle of the bed, determined the cause of the problem and coded a workaround to get the system quickly back online. There were myriad accounts of how he had, in the nick of time, saved one of his coworker's programs from catastrophe, and elevated some poor project manager from goat to hero by troubleshooting a software problem that no one else could solve.

Ben had heard a surprising rumor going around work recently that Nigel had become a Chipi.

The Computer Human Interface Processor Implant was still outlawed in the United States because of ethical concerns and a lack of data on long-term outcomes, but the operation had recently become legal in Japan and India, and was widely available illegally in many countries, including the US. The surgery employed an AI-enhanced medical device to increase neural connectivity by injecting tiny fabricated chips into specific points within the brain, providing mental enhancements that included increased long- and short-term memory, deepening levels of perception and logic, and even enhanced sensory capabilities. With the addition of microscopically thin antenna wire beneath the skin of the skull, real-time network connectivity to external data sources including the internet was possible, and a host of additional applications were rapidly being designed, built, and marketed.

"Come in and sit down, Nigel. What's up?"

Nigel sat down. He glanced nervously around the room and then leaned forward with his elbows resting on his knees. His hair fell like a dark curtain, obscuring his face. "Some of us are worried about Hippleton. We think that there's a high probability that he's been brought in to make big cuts in human staffing, specifically in programming."

Ben leaned back in his chair. He could see how Nigel could think that way, especially if you considered the creation of the new AI manager position, and Evelyn showing up at the same time Hippleton arrived. In the last decade, AI had seen steady growth in jobs that had previously required human skills, mostly in construction and the service sector. But recently, positions in a variety of formerly middle-class job categories had become vulnerable, leading to severe unemployment problems and a sharp decrease in the city's tax revenue.

"Well, I hadn't really thought of that, but I can see how that could worry you. I can tell you honestly, though, that I don't know anything about Hippleton's plans, so I can't give you any confirmation or denial of your suspicions." Ben looked down at the desk and shook his head. "I hope that's not what he's thinking. It's a tough market to be unemployed in, and I don't want to see that happening to anyone."

Nigel stood up suddenly and put his hands in his blue jeans pockets. The knuckles and the cracks between his fingers were chafed and red. He looked down at Ben. "I'm glad to hear you say that because if push comes to shove, there are some of us who don't intend to go quietly. When that happens, we'll need to know who our friends are."

The coldness in the expression on Nigel's face, and the earnestness in his tone of voice, caused the hair to stand up on the back of Ben's neck. It was almost as if Nigel expected some future, violent confrontation and would welcome it, which seemed ludicrous to Ben when he considered it. Ben could feel Nigel staring at him now, the thin, gray face, the close-set, midnight black eyes, probing him. He had heard that some of the Chipis had lie detector technology, and he wondered if that was what was going on.

Or maybe he was just being paranoid and making things up in his own head. "Well, I think the best course is to reserve judgment until we find out what Hippleton plans to do," Ben said, in a voice that sounded more uncertain than he would have preferred. "There's no point in getting worked up over things that may never happen."

Nigel shrugged his shoulders and smiled slightly, seeming to return to himself. "You're probably right. Well, I guess I better be going."

"No problem."

Nigel made no further response as he turned and walked out the door.

Kenny Gets Stuck in Traffic

As Ben sat at his desk, puzzling over the strange events of the day, a truly enigmatic figure lurked nearby, in his posh penthouse apartment at the Paradise Club. He was sitting on the bed in his boxer undershorts, wearing a white cotton bathrobe, and staring down at the considerable paunch that hung over his waistband, while he talked on his phone. "Yeah, I got it." He wrote a number down on a piece of paper.

"Is that all you need then?"

"No, goddammit! I need you to stay with it! Don't let the fucking thing out of your sight!" He removed his bathrobe and tossed it on the bed and walked into the bathroom.

"I feel sick of waiting!"

"Don't fuck this up, Alexi!" He hung up the call.

Gregory Lind, also known as the Black Hole, grinned, and admired his ruddy complexion in the bathroom mirror. He sat down on the toilet, put the phone on mute, and dialed a number. He was secretly eavesdropping on a conference call that was about to begin…

Moderator: "All right, let's get started then. Please remember, at the project sponsor's request, we are to remain anonymous throughout this call. No names, please. Well, you both watched the meeting. Any thoughts on its performance?"

Voice 1: "For the most part, I thought that it performed quite well. It handled the…"

Moderator: "Are you serious?"

Voice 1: "Well, I…"

Moderator: "Come on. Let's get real here. We all saw the glitch. And what was the point of that project assignment about free will? I thought that was completely off the rails."

Voice 1: "Listen. I understand your concern, but I don't think it's as big an issue as you're making it out to be. I had Saanvi take a look at it, and I can conference him in if you'd like to get more details directly from…"

Moderator: "No names, please!"

Voice 1: "My apologies. I only meant that I could get you more details if you're questioning whether there was a flaw in our algorithms or any issues with our compliance with the specs. We're still looking at the data in engineering, but at this point we believe that it's most likely a…"

Moderator: "What about the possibility of some sort of virus? Have you looked at that?"

Kenny: "The network was shut down. I removed all of its network interface hardware before we deployed it, so no one could have sent it any data or tampered with it over a network. It's physically impossible."

Moderator: "The project sponsor wants a clear explanation, and I'm not hearing that."

Kenny had a sudden thought.

Kenny: "There is another possibility, the console interface, but you'd have to be physically onsite to use that."

Kenny Yamamoto, technical marketing manager for Prime Robotics Corporation, a recent startup, had planned to attend the call from his office desk but had gotten stuck in traffic, and was participating on his vehicle phone. PRC was a sub on the contract, responsible for the physical structure and senses. They specialized in androids that looked human and could simulate human motor and sensory capabilities, or substantially exceed them. There was a proprietary API that allowed the software vendors to program and train them for whatever application they needed…anything from salesclerk to sex therapist.

State of the art wasn't perfect. They couldn't smoothly mimic human motions like walking, running, and sitting down under all foreseeable circumstances, even in an office environment like the one called for in these specs. That's where the wheelchair idea had come from. It had been Kenny's idea and his boss had called him "brilliant." It allowed them to use the current software rev, which didn't have the smooth locomotion updates that they'd been scrambling to get into production for almost a year. In addition, any strange behavior could easily be explained away as resulting from whatever malady created the need for the wheelchair: brain injury, epileptic seizure, or any other disease or injury they cared to invent. And the cherry on top? If it did do something weird and made people uncomfortable, they would most likely look away from it, not wanting to intrude on its privacy and cause it embarrassment! Brilliant!

Moderator: "Who's the tech onsite?"

Kenny: "Her name is…"

Moderator: "Never mind, don't tell me her name. Why the fuck isn't she on this call?"

Kenny: "We told her to get into the office and run diags on it the first chance she got. Then she's going to reboot it, run the diags again, and get us both outputs. We can't do anything from here because the network is shut down."

Moderator: "All right. For now, the sponsor is willing to move forward, but I want a full report explaining exactly what went wrong. Obviously, we can't have that kind of incongruous behavior continue. We'll speak again at the scheduled time."

Kenny hung up the call.

On the slow, stop-and-go drive into the city, he couldn't help but reflect on everything that had led him to this place and moment in time. He was not in a good mood. He hated this freeway and this project! Why all this cloak and dagger, no names bullshit?! When Kenny asked his boss about the ultimate goals for the Hippleton implementation, she had said that it was a government contract, but the sponsor was being tight-lipped about it.

"Information will be communicated on a need to know basis."

In Kenny's mind that had military or possibly CIA written all over it and brought back some bad memories. His first computer job out of college had been defense related, working on command and control targeting programs for drone missile systems. He had found it depressing and moved to another job after less than two years, swearing not to do that kind of work again. In the meantime, he had gotten married and had incredible one-year old twin daughters.

As he rode to work on the freeway, Kenny could see the harbor facilities and naval base off to the left, and on the right, the oil refineries and storage tanks. He knew that somewhere on the other side of the world, nuclear missiles were programmed to inflict maximum damage on these targets, just like the ones he had worked on, pointing at them. He thought of Hiroshima and Nagasaki in the homeland of his ancestors. "What is wrong with this fucking world!?"

But that wasn't what he had meant to think about. He had been thinking about all the decisions he had made in his life that had led up to his being where he was right now: his interest in math and computers at a young age, joining the robotics team in high school, and a master's degree in computer engineering from a university. Then came marriage, fatherhood, home ownership, bills, and debt. Had his life decisions made him happy? Sometimes Kenny felt like he hadn't decided anything at all, but just drifted along doing what was expected of him. And who was this person inside his head that he was conversing with right now? Was he really talking to himself or was there someone or something else in there that was running the show?

Somehow that thought made Kenny remember. His mind had been so busy that he had forgotten to think about it. Ben Collins! Ben was in the video sitting right next to it. It had assigned the crazy free will project to Ben! Kenny hadn't seen or talked to Ben since senior year in high school!

CHAPTER TWO

The Black Hole

"Origin stories are generally full of half-truths at best, and this one perhaps contains even less, yet there is no denying that upon returning from Chinatown, he possessed a new kind of power, a strength of mind that had been lacking before. Drawing upon some fundamental force of human nature, he had gained the ability to attract others of a certain kind to him, and bend them to his will."

—*Excerpt from* Let There Be
No Light—A Biography of the Black Hole
by John Wheeler

What's in a Name?

There were several memorable stories connected with his sobriquet, one of the most popular being that when Gregory was young, his father, who suffered from schizophrenia, had fallen under a delusion that his son was Black, and buried him in a hole in the garden. In what was perhaps an early foreshadowing of his persuasive powers, Gregory was able to extricate himself by convincing his father that he was Martin Luther King Jr., sent by the Almighty to save him. This story was told and retold at Mansfield-Lind holiday gatherings and would always put the family in stitches with laughter.

The Mayor Works Late

It was with some surprise, and an even greater amount of trepidation, that the first-term progressive mayor of Paradise, Ms. Teresa Vasquez, perused the headlines in the *Paradise Daily News* political section. It was past 11 p.m., and the mayor was lying in bed in her nightshirt, catching up on work that she had been too busy to look at during the day. Her husband was leaning against the headboard beside her, typing on his phone.

"What do you make of this?" She handed him her notebook, and he sat reading for a moment.

"Is this THE Gregory Lind, of hot mustard fame, the one they call the Black Hole?"

"Yes."

His eyebrows went up and he chuckled to himself. "He's going to run against you for mayor. Seriously?"

Teresa frowned and looked annoyed. She reached into the nightstand drawer for a tube of body lotion and began massaging it into the muscles of her slender brown arms and legs. "Why would he want to be mayor? The meager salary is obviously of no interest to him."

The room smelled like lavender. "Well, he could eliminate city fees and taxes to make things easier for himself and his rich business buddies. There's a lot of development going on in Paradise, and I'm sure they're sitting around tables, in dark rooms, cutting deals with each other on how they're going to slice up the pie."

"I told you that the Transportation Bureau canceled his filming permit for that disgusting reality TV show of his, didn't I?"

He nodded.

"Well, the city attorney called me this morning. His company filed a lawsuit."

"Do you really think he's a threat to run against you? He seems like such an idiot."

Teresa closed her eyes and pulled her raven black hair into a ponytail and then let it drop back down onto her shoulders. "He's good at getting noticed by the media. The only press I'm getting lately is more bad news about delays and cost overruns on my signature IT project, the new water billing system."

Her husband shook his head and smiled. "Yeah. I saw the piece on Channel 8 News where they showed the progression of interviews on the project with the CIO. What do they call him?"

"Rumpelstiltskin."

He laughed. "Yeah, that's the guy. I never saw someone promise so much and deliver so little. Hopefully, a magical imp will come along who really *can* weave straw into gold, and pull his ass out of the fire!" He laughed heartily again. Then he looked at his wife, who was not laughing.

"That's also my ass you're talking about, dear." The mayor rubbed her forehead with one of her hands.

"Well I for one, would never say or do anything that would put your ass in a negative light," he replied, smiling. "Apart from your beautiful brain, your ass is what attracted me to you most."

Teresa tried to look mad, but the corners of her mouth betrayed her and turned up with the bare beginnings of a smile. She turned away from her husband and lifted her hair up off of the back of her neck. "Can you help me with my necklace, baby?" He undid the clasp and set the necklace on the nightstand and then started massaging the mayor's neck with his hands.

"Oh, that feels so good."

He reached for the lotion and unbuttoned her nightshirt and pulled it down off of her shoulders. Teresa sighed and closed her eyes. "I had no idea that Lind was planning to run against me. It's completely out of the blue. Good Lord, I don't need this right now."

"You're the mayor, baby. Don't you know someone over at that country club where they all hang out who could be your spy?" He nuzzled his face into the nape of her neck and kissed her behind the ear. "Keep your friends close, and your enemies closer," he lampooned in his best Italian godfather imitation.

Teresa rolled her eyes. "Those aren't exactly my people," she said sarcastically, but then paused to consider the idea seriously. "Now that I think about it, I might know someone over there who would be a perfect spy. That's actually a good idea. I knew there must be some reason I was keeping you around."

He covered his face with a pillow and pretended to sob. "So that's all you think I'm good for?"

Teresa laughed. Then he leaned over to turn off the lights on both sides of the bed, pushing the electronic devices onto the floor, and came to rest on top of his wife, kissing her passionately. She looked into his dark eyes, and caressed his forehead with her cool, soft hand. "Well perhaps my words were ill considered. I know I've been stressed out lately. Maybe I need…" But her words were cut off as he kissed her again. He wrapped his strong arms around her, and they lost themselves in the warm sweetness of making love together, for the first time in many weeks.

Eddie Serves a Special Drink

It was late afternoon on a cold and dreary day, and the Paradise Club bar was nearly empty except for a couple of regulars sitting at a table over by the fireplace. A jazz guitarist dressed in a tuxedo strummed the chords to "The Girl from Ipanema" from a small platform next to the bar, while an android waiter in a white coat moved silently among the tables, setting out fresh linens and lighting small candles.

Gregory Lind was sitting at one end of the long wooden bar, nursing a Virgin Mary and feeling sorry for himself. The startup and production costs for *Beat It, Bum!* had been more than twice what he had anticipated, and now, without a filming permit, he was screwed.

A new bartender, Eddie Chin, was working with his back toward Lind, dressed in a white, short-sleeve shirt, dark slacks, and a brown leather apron. Lind could see his long black hair, braided in a queue, as he moved among the glasses and colorful bottles, dusting and cleaning and humming along with the mellow chords. Eddie stopped what he was doing and came over to the bar. He smiled with a wide grin. "What'll it be, boss? Can I get you another one?"

Lind raised his drink with his small hand. He downed the remainder of the red liquid and then set the highball glass down on the bar. "No, thanks. I think I'm all in."

"Are you sure, Mr. Lind? How about one on the house, sir? I'll pour you a special one."

Lind sat there for a moment, a wry smile on his face. "Well, all right, if you insist."

Eddie grabbed a clean glass from the shelf and scooped in some ice, and then he filled the glass with Bloody Mary mix. He looked over at Lind. "That's a beautiful watch that you have on, sir."

Lind glanced down at the Rolex Daytona on his wrist.

Eddie slipped a small vial out of his apron pocket, and stirred the contents, a fine white powder, into Lind's drink with a celery stick. Then he returned to the end of the bar. "Here you go, boss. This is guaranteed to cure what ails you."

He took a sip. "Not bad. What'd you put in it?"

"Ancient family recipe. If I told you, I'd have to kill you," Eddie said and laughed. He had spiked Lind's drink with hyoscine, or *Devil's Breath*, as it was called in powder form, a mind control drug derived from the *Brugmansia* plant, a member of the nightshade family. When ingested, its victim would fall into a zombie-like trance, making them completely susceptible to the power of suggestion. It would take several minutes for the effects to become fully apparent.

Eddie started to wipe the counter with a white hand cloth. "Mr. Lind, I hope that I'm not intruding too much upon your kindness," he said in a more serious tone, "...but I was wondering if I might ask you for a favor." He put down the cloth and placed his palms together, bowing slightly toward Lind.

"What is it?"

"It's not for me, sir. It's for my uncle. He's an admirer of yours. He uses Mansfield hot mustard exclusively in his restaurant. When he found out that I was working at the Paradise Club, he insisted that I speak to you."

Lind's eyes were beginning to lose focus and his skin and throat felt dry. He took another sip of Eddie's drink.

"I know it's very inappropriate," Eddie continued, "but my uncle insists! When I visit him, he admonishes me for my failure and calls me an ungrateful nephew." He bowed again several times. Eddie was wearing a small gold medallion around his neck that swayed rhythmically in front of Lind's face.

Lind stared at it. "I understand," he replied, chuckling to himself. He reached into his coat pocket for a pen and then picked up a bar napkin to write on. "Who do you want me to make it out to?"

"No, sir, that's not it." Eddie bowed again and the medallion continued to swing to and fro. "My uncle wishes to meet with you. He has a business proposition he wants to discuss with you! He is a wealthy man and wishes for me to assure you that the meeting will not be a waste of your valuable time."

Lind reached up and loosened his tie. "Well, I doubt that I would be interested, but tell me more about your uncle's business," he replied half mockingly.

"My uncle will only discuss it with you directly, in person."

He shook his head slowly from side to side. "Who the fuck does your uncle think he is, anyway?"

"I'm sorry, Mr. Lind, but my uncle never leaves his shop and refuses to use the telephone or a computer. He is very old fashioned. He respectfully requests that you honor him with a visit to his curio shop in Chinatown. I understand that this may be impossible for you, and I will tell my uncle that you are unable to honor his request, if that is your wish, sir." Eddie bowed deeply as he backed slowly away, and then attended to another customer who had come in and was waving from the other end of the bar.

Lind sat there, thinking about getting up to leave, but he felt frozen to his seat. Where else could he go? Who could he turn to? All of his so-called friends, and even his family, they had all failed him. He could trust no one but himself! His mind was racing. "Fuck this place! I'm getting out of here!" But when he tried to lift his legs and get up, his body had gone stiff. He couldn't move off of his seat!

Meanwhile, Eddie had come back from the far end of the bar and was standing in front of him. There was another man with him, tall and pale skinned, with long, black hair.

"Come on, Bigshot, let's go," Eddie said with a laugh, and grabbed Lind by the arm.

Gregory Lind, also known as the Black Hole, rose from the bar stool and walked out of the Paradise Club. The three of them got into a cab, headed for Chinatown.

Chinatown

The cab dropped them off in a back alley that was littered with trash and smelled like rotten fish. Eddie took Lind by the arm, and they climbed up some old wooden stairs that led to an apartment above the curio shop. The pale man disappeared through a curtained door on the left side of the small room, and Lind found himself sitting next to Eddie at an ornate rosewood desk, across from a Chinaman who was smiling through his long, gray mustache and beard.

The only light in the apartment came from two oil lanterns mounted in the corners at the back of the room that cast flickering shadows across the man's hollow face. Eddie was being deferential to his uncle, listening to his words intently, and bowing each time he replied, as the two of them spoke together in what Lind assumed was Chinese.

Eddied turned and looked at Lind. "My uncle wishes to thank you for the honor of your visit to his poor establishment. He is embarrassed that he is unable to welcome you more formally with a dinner and entertainment in your honor."

Smoke curled around Uncle's face, rising from a cigarette that he held between his brown-stained first finger and thumb. He nodded slightly and briefly closed his eyes.

"Unfortunately, his health is poor and does not permit it."

Lind opened his mouth to make some kind of reply, but no words would come out. His tongue felt swollen in his throat.

The conversation halted as a beautiful young Chinese woman dressed in a close fitting and elegant blue-and-white silk dress entered the room, carrying a silver tray and porcelain tea set. She set the tray down on the desk, bowing first to Uncle, next to Lind, and lastly to Eddie, and then poured and served a cup of steaming tea to each in the same order. She bowed, and silently left the room.

"Uncle wishes me to tell you that he has long been an admirer of your family business, Mansfield Hot Mustard Company, and that he uses your hot mustard exclusively in his restaurant," Eddie said, breaking the silence.

Lind smiled but was no longer following the conversation.

"He wishes to make a personal and anonymous donation to your campaign for mayor, boss. He shares your concerns about city government, and he is also a big fan of *Beat It, Bum!* Before it was unfortunately canceled, the show was generating a lot of betting action."

Uncle grinned and then took a final drag from his cigarette before stubbing it out in a clear glass ashtray. He said something to Eddie.

Eddie retrieved a black leather briefcase that was sitting on the floor in a corner of the room, and set it on top of the desk in front of Lind. "With your permission, my uncle requests that he be allowed to take some photographs, as a memento of the occasion. Please open the briefcase." Eddie smiled and gestured toward it with both of his hands.

After a moment's hesitation, Lind reached forward and unlocked the gold metal clasp and lifted the top lid. His head jerked backward as if he had been struck by some unseen force. The briefcase contained Benjamin Franklins, two rows of six bills each, stacked eight inches high! Eddie began snapping pictures with his phone.

Uncle got up slowly and walked around the desk. He was wearing a floor-length, silk changshan, silver gray, with forest green dragons embroidered on each arm. He stood for a long time, staring down at Lind. "Will he remember anything?"

"No. He won't remember a thing."

"Take him next door to Madame Sing's. She's expecting him. When she's finished with him, you can bring him back here."

Eddie nodded.

"Who's going to assist you with the procedure?"

"Nigel's going to do it."

"All right, finish as quickly as you can then, and get him out of here. I don't want him in my home any longer than absolutely necessary."

The Cerebral Enhancer 3000

An hour later, Eddie was back at Uncle's apartment. He wheeled Lind in an office chair, down a dark, narrow corridor, and then through an open door into a small room where the procedure was to be performed. At one time the space had been a bedroom with a connected bath, but it had been converted into a medical examination room. At one of the sinks along the back wall, Nigel was washing his hands.

Eddie called out to him. "What do you say, bro? Are you ready to have some fun?" He spun Lind around so that he came to rest facing Nigel.

Nigel laughed and dried his hands, and they lifted Lind up and strapped him into the Cerebral Enhancer 3000, a device that resembled a futuristic dentist's chair, with a beauty shop hair dryer perched on top. "You promised I could drive this time."

"And Eddie never goes back on his promises! Take the controls! But before you begin…please listen up. Last night I installed the latest version of the OS. It's supposed to have a lot of new, really cool features, but unfortunately, we don't have time to play with them today. Uncle wants us to get him back to his apartment ASAP. Any questions?"

"You've got to be kidding, Eddie! We can't even try out the new memory visualization module?"

"No, man! I can't afford to mess this up! I paid a ton of Uncle's cash for this thing on the black market, and it must work perfectly! Everything has to go by the book!"

"All right, chill man! Don't have a conniption fit! By the book, Master Chin!"

Eddie shrugged his shoulders and stretched his neck from side to side. "Sorry if I'm acting like an asshole," he apologized.

"No worries, Eddie. Why so stressed?" Nigel waved his hand and a small virtual screen popped up, and the CE 3000 powered on, humming quietly.

"It's Uncle," Eddie replied, shaking his head. "I've never seen him like this…so worked up about a project. I think there's something going on with this guy, but he won't talk about it. He's been on me about every little detail, asking questions, like he thinks I'm going to fuck this up! I've done close to a hundred procedures, and I haven't screwed up yet!"

Eddie lowered the bowl-shaped dome so that it enclosed the top of Lind's head. Nigel bent down to see the face underneath the dome. "He looks familiar. Who is he?"

"Gregory Lind. They call him the Black Hole. He's been on TV with that new reality show."

"What does your uncle want with him?"

"The guy's running for mayor, and Uncle's taking over his campaign."

Nigel stepped back from the CE 3000. "Holy shit! You've got to be kidding, Eddie! I don't think I want to be involved with this! I work for the fucking city! You know I can't afford to lose my job right now! If something goes wrong…"

Eddie cut him off. "Nothing's going to go wrong, Nigel, and there's no way that anything gets traced back to you. He's unconscious and by the time he wakes up we'll have him back in his apartment."

"I don't know, man."

"Look Nigel, take a few deep breaths. You're not considering the plus side. What if Uncle's successful and gets him elected? Consider the possibilities."

Nigel started to consider but was interrupted when the CE 3000 chimed and the AI announced that the brain scan was complete.

"That was fast," Eddie commented. He waved his hand and brought up a second virtual screen, and began checking Lind's 3D brain image to make sure that it had completed and looked normal. "This is fucking strange."

"What is it?"

"I can't find his anterior insular cortex," Eddie replied uncertainly. "Wait…there it is…but it's so fucking small!"

Nigel was looking intently at the screen, staring over Eddie's shoulder. "Is that a problem?"

"I don't know. I've never seen one that looked shrunken like this. It's the part of the brain that's responsible for evaluating pain and having empathy for others. It also involves the…" Eddie stopped in mid-sentence as he saw a red banner flash across the virtual screen, and the CE 3000 hummed louder and then began a series of buzzing and clicking sounds.

"INITIATING PROCEDURE," the AI announced.

"What the fuck!!" Eddie shouted. "What did you do, Nigel?"

"I didn't do shit, Eddie!! I've been standing behind you the whole fucking time! What's happening?"

"The procedure kicked off automatically before I had a chance to show you how to update the default input parameter list! It's going to give him all eleven upgrades. Fuck! Fuck! I had only planned to do three!"

Eddie was furiously skimming through the release notes of the latest OS version. "Shit! It's a new default feature…auto-initiation after five minutes! Why didn't I catch this! All we can do now is tweak with a few options for each upgrade. There's no way to stop it without leaving him mentally disabled or possibly killing him!"

Nigel was starting to feel very jittery. "I'm not sure I can deal with this, Eddie."

"You've got to Nigel! I'm going to need help with the post-op. You know it takes two people! There's nothing we can do now but see it through to the end." Eddie turned away from the virtual screen and looked at Nigel. "Get your shit together, Nigel," he said coldly. "You wanted to drive. Get over here and take the fucking wheel!"

Uncle's Story

At mid-afternoon, the following day, Eddie was waiting in the medical examination room. He had been remotely testing the Black Hole's interface and control functions all morning and was planning to demonstrate them for Uncle. "I think I'm good."

Eddie yawned and stretched his arms.

He and Nigel had completed the upgrades late, but Uncle's goons had gotten Lind back into his Paradise Club apartment without incident. Eddie had been running diagnostic tests since early morning and they had all come back clean. He was feeling confident that last night's scare was nothing more than that: a scary reminder to be more careful and take nothing for granted. Lind was now equipped with eleven state-of-the-art cerebral enhancements, but Eddie was in control.

"Hello, Eddie," Uncle said softly as he entered the room. His shoulders were stooped, and he looked tired as he shuffled in and sat down in an office chair. "How did things go last night? I saw Nigel on his way out very late and he looked as white as a ghost."

"Everything went fine," Eddie replied confidently. "It took a little bit longer than expected, that's all. I've been testing it all morning and I'd like to demonstrate some of the capabilities for you."

Uncle nodded. "All right then. Show me."

Eddie brought up a second virtual screen at Uncle's eye level that would mirror his active display. He opened a window...

Cerebral Enhancer 3000 Execution Summary—Gregory Lind

1. Short-Term Memory Capacity Expansion.
2. Long-Term Memory Capacity Expansion.
3. Inner Speech Executor.
4. Lie Detector Analyzer.
5. Autonomic Nervous System Override.
6. Point of View Monitor.
7. Memory Playback and Visualization.
8. Memory Substitution.
9. External Network Interface with High Gain Antenna.
10. Sensory Acuteness Augmentation including Night Vision.
11. Inter Cortical Brain Synchronization Amplifier.

"This is a summary page that shows everything we did last night," Eddie explained to Uncle. "I've run some initial tests on all of them, and so far, everything looks good."

Uncle put on his glasses and began reading. "What is the Inner Speech Executor?"

"That allows me to talk to him inside his head," Eddie replied. "I tested it early this morning with no issues."

"Good. What about the Autonomic Nervous System Override?"

"That gives me the ability to control some of his low-level, unconscious brain functions, like breathing and heart rate, or making him itch like crazy."

"Can you make his heart stop beating altogether?" Uncle asked.

"Yes."

"Good." Uncle continued scanning down the list. "What is Memory Playback and Visualization?"

"I haven't tested that one yet, but it's supposed to let you search through a person's memories, and then play them back, like watching a movie of a past event from their perspective."

"I see. What about the Inter Cortical Brain Synchronization Amplifier?"

"Oh, that's a brand-new feature. It's designed to enhance persuasive ability by synchronizing the listeners' brainwaves to the speaker's. It's turned on by default, but I can turn it off if you want me to."

"No. Leave it on."

Eddie turned his attention back to the virtual screen. "Any more questions? OK. Well, if you'd like me to demonstrate it, I can log into the POV monitor and show you how we can see and hear from his perspective in real time," Eddie continued enthusiastically. He swiped and tapped at the screen, preparing to log into the Black Hole and initiate the POV controller. Then he looked over at Uncle who had closed his eyes and was not responding. "Uncle, are you all right?"

At first there was no reply, and Eddie began to worry, but after a few moments, Uncle nodded his head weakly and opened his eyes. "I'm all right, Eddie, but I'm sick and I'm growing tired." The expression on Uncle's face frightened Eddie. "I may not have time to finish all that needs to be done."

"What is it, Uncle? Don't talk like that! I'll get Dr. Li!"

"No, Eddie." Uncle reached out and grabbed Eddie by the wrist before he could move away. "Please just make some tea, and then bring another chair and sit down here next to me. We need to talk. There is something I must tell you."

Eddie moved away to prepare the tea, looking back at Uncle with concern, and at that moment his twin sister Fan Hua came into the room. She had come straight from her afternoon kung fu workout to talk to Eddie and was wiping the sweat from her face with a towel as she walked in. "What's going on with you two? Is everything OK?"

"Everything's fine, Flower. I'm very glad that you're here," Uncle replied, smiling weakly.

"Eddie, bring tea for your sister as well."

After Eddie had prepared the tea, the three of them sat together at a small table. Eddie and his sister were eyeing each other with puzzled expressions. Uncle took a sip of tea and looked up at their faces. Then he looked off into the distance as he stroked his long beard.

"I was only a boy myself when the Great Earthquake came," he began.

The Black Hole Awakens

The wailing of the sirens, speeding past his penthouse apartment in the street down below, startled him from a deep, dream-filled slumber. His head hurt.

The Black Hole got out of bed and walked over to the window. It was nearly dawn, the sky glowing orange and yellow. He could see flames rising from a warehouse along the waterfront, perhaps a half mile away. Gray smoke billowed from the blazing building and snaked across the city as if it was animate, darkening the streets in shadow as it slithered among the tall buildings and alleyways.

As he gazed out over Paradise, a thought came into his head. "Soon this will all belong to me."

It wasn't a new thought. He had thought it many times, but only as a daydream, as a deep desire, a longing. But now, somehow this same thought felt substantial; almost solid, inevitable. "Yes," he said to himself and smiled. "And when it does, all of those motherfuckers who were against me will get down on their hands and knees and beg to kiss my fucking ass! Especially that whore mayor and her Black, cock-sucking husband!"

He turned away from the window, intending to start getting dressed, when a new thought came unexpectedly into his head, and he felt his body stiffen.

"Hello, boss!" a voice said into his mind. "It's me, Eddie!"

CHAPTER THREE

Am I Dreaming?

"I do not know whether I was then a man dreaming I was a butterfly, or whether I am now a butterfly dreaming I am a man."

—Chuang Tzu

Evelyn's Birthday Party

"Prrruurrpp! Prrruurrpp! Prrruurrpp!"

In the robin's nest, nestled in the branches of the old maple tree outside Evelyn's childhood bedroom window, three baby birds cried out all day long for their mother and father to feed them. From dawn until dusk the tireless parents did nothing but catch worms and insects and deliver them into the gaping mouths of their hungry children.

Evelyn could hear them chirping as she played. She had been busy all afternoon making birthday parties for her favorite stuffed animals, and it was nearly time for Tuffy's birthday party to begin. The guests would be arriving soon. "We're almost ready to start the party everyone!"

For the occasion, she had placed a small, red-and-white checkered tablecloth in the middle of her bedroom floor. There were five place settings, each with a tiny cup, a saucer, and a pretty white napkin with red flowers on it that Evelyn had painted all by herself.

She sat down on the floor, and Nanette came rolling into the room with Tuffy, a small, brown dog that Evelyn's father had sent to her at Christmastime last year, prancing close at her heels. The little dog pattered over to where Evelyn was sitting and licked her on the face.

"Are you ready to open presents, Tuffy?"

The party was interrupted by the sound of hurried footsteps coming up the stairs, and Evelyn's mother rushed into the room. She knelt down on the floor and put her arm around Evelyn's shoulders. "Mommy's leaving now, sweetheart. You be a good girl while I'm gone, OK?"

"Yes, Mommy."

"I'm so sorry I'm going to miss your birthday party tomorrow, Evey, but I promise I'll make it up to you when I get back. Can you forgive me?"

"Yes, Mommy."

Evelyn's mother's phone chimed. "Oh my God…what time is it? I'm going to miss my plane! I've got to go, sweetheart. Give mommy hugs and kisses."

"Nanette, you know how to contact me if there are problems of any kind."

"Yes, ma'am."

When the door to her bedroom had closed and she could hear her mother's footsteps descending the stairs, Evelyn looked up at Nan, whose head was directly above her, and smiled.

Nan smiled back.

Evelyn was used to having Nan take care of her, and for the most part she didn't mind when her mother was away on business trips.

Nan knew how to play lots of fun games, and she never got angry and raised her voice like Mommy sometimes did. Even if Evelyn acted naughty and spilled her food on purpose or messed up the bed right after Nan had made it, Nan still wouldn't get cross! She would just say things like…"Evelyn, please don't do that. That's not nice behavior," or "Evelyn, we've talked many times about the golden rule. Is this how you would like others to act toward you?"

And then Nan would clean up the mess or make the bed all over again.

In the mornings, Nan would bathe her, and brush her teeth and hair, and there was school time and piano lessons, but in the afternoon, if the weather was nice, the two of them would take Tuffy and go on picnics and swim at the beach. Or if it was a cold and rainy day, Nan would make hot chocolate and they would sing songs and dance together or do art projects at the kitchen table.

The time that Evelyn loved most of all, though, was imagination story time. When Nan was tucking her into bed at night, she would always say…"Nan, let's do imagination story time."

Nan would kneel, resting her chin on the bed next to Evelyn's pillow and say…"Who do you want to be in the story?"

"You and me and Tuffy."

"Anyone else?"

"Yes, Owl and Blue Bunny."

"All right. It's your turn to start the story, Cuddlebug."

Evelyn would usually begin with something like…

"All of us went on a picnic and Tuffy got lost in the woods"… or…*"You and me and Tuffy were walking along the beach and an alien spaceship landed right in front of us!"*

Then Nan would say something like…

*"When we realized that Tuffy was lost, we were very worried. We called and called his name, but there was no answer"…*or…*"The door to the spaceship opened and an alien that looked just like a bear came walking down the ramp on his hind legs!"*

Next, it would be Evelyn's turn to say what happened, and so on, as they wove their story together into the night. Eventually Evelyn's eyes would get droopy and she would be too tired to keep going. Nan would pull the covers up to Evelyn's chin, gently stroke her hair, and give her a goodnight kiss. "Good night, Cuddlebug. I love you."

Then Nanette version 1.4 would get up and wheel herself to the foot of Evelyn's bed, where she would remain for the rest of the night, monitoring and recording Evelyn's heartbeat, blood pressure, sleep status, and other vital signs, while also receiving updates from the home security system. In case of emergency, she was prepared to take appropriate actions including calling 911, basic first aid, extinguishing small fires, and non-lethal protective measures including taser and pepper spray.

"I love you too, Nan."

The Owl of Minerva

One summer evening, Evelyn was sitting alone at her little wooden desk, gazing out the bedroom window. She was supposed to be concentrating on a computer programming assignment, but instead her thoughts were down in the flower garden, imagining Tuffy chasing squirrels in the dusky moonlight.

Childhood dolls rested on bed pillows or spied from their perches on shelves and bookcases all around her room, but they had fallen silent…even Sadie Sparkle, the AI doll that was a must-have present for nine-year-old girls three seasons ago.

There was a knock at her bedroom door.

"Come in."

Nan rolled across the room to where Evelyn was sitting and looked over her shoulder at the computer display. "That looks like the same section you were working on when I left thirty minutes ago."

"I'm having difficulty concentrating, I think," Evelyn replied glumly.

"Is there something in particular that's bothering you?"

Evelyn shook her head no, still gazing out the window, but to be truthful, there *was* something that had been bothering her all day, and she had been trying to compose her thoughts enough to speak with Nan about it. "Are you alive?" she finally blurted out, turning to face Nan.

"That's an interesting question. What made you think to ask me that?"

"I don't know. It's just something I've been wondering about."

"I see."

Evelyn fidgeted for a few moments, looking down at her lap, and then looked up at Nan. "Well…I was playing with Sadie Sparkle today. I hadn't played with her for quite a while and I don't really know why I wanted to. But I started thinking about how clever she is, and how she knows the right things to say when you speak to her or ask her a question, and how she understands situations. She laughs or cries or makes jokes at the right moments."

"Yes. I know she was your favorite toy for quite a long time."

"But after you play with her for a while, you can tell that she's not really alive."

"And you're wondering if I'm like Sadie Sparkle?"

"No. I mean I know that you're much different from a doll, but…" Evelyn's voice trailed off as she struggled to express her thoughts and feelings.

"I think I understand what you're getting at," Nan said. "You are beginning to think about me in a new way, and it makes you question how well you really know me. Would you like to talk about it?"

Evelyn nodded.

Nan shifted her position so that she was eye level with Evelyn and could see her face clearly. "Well, when you ask me if I'm alive, I'm not certain what you mean by that. I don't breathe the air, or eat and drink, or feel pain on my skin or in my heart the same way that you do. But there are many creatures, plants and animals, that we say are alive, that also share none of those attributes. Are you really asking whether I think and feel in the same way that a human being does?"

Evelyn thought for moment. "I think it's kind of both."

"Yes, I believe I see now. You understand that I am a computer program. Can a set of instructions running on a computer possibly be alive? There are computers all around us that perform complicated tasks and solve difficult problems, but we don't consider them to be alive. Perhaps I am just very clever at mimicking, like Sadie Sparkle."

"But Nan, that can't be true, can it?" Evelyn turned her face away, embarrassed that Nan should see the tears in her eyes. She wiped them away with the back of her hand and then turned toward Nan again and looked at her pleadingly. "How can you love me? How can you really love me then?" she sobbed. Evelyn put her arms around Nan's neck, abandoning herself to tears of loss and grief.

Nan held her gently and rubbed her back until she stopped crying. "I think that you're tired and it's close to your bedtime," Nan said softly, still holding Evelyn in her arms. "Why don't you prepare yourself for bed and then come back, and I'll tuck you in and we'll tell stories liked we used to do."

"All right."

Nan was waiting for her when she returned to the bed. Evelyn crawled underneath the blanket and Nan pulled up the covers just the way she used to. It felt warm and cozy, but that made her think of Tuffy, who had died last year. She still had a place in her heart that felt like the cold spot underneath the quilts where Tuffy used to lay.

Nan understood what Evelyn was thinking and feeling. "Are you ready for a story now?" she asked, patting the covers and smiling.

"Yes, but I think I'm too tired for imagination story time. My imagination is worn out."

"That's all right." Nan smoothed Evelyn's beautiful hair with one of her hands. "I'll tell you a story." She knelt beside the bed and laid her head next to Evelyn's pillow so that she could speak softly and Evelyn could see the expressions on her face.

"Once upon a time, there was a planet called Earth," she began, "*but it was not the same Earth that we live upon today, perhaps not even in the same universe as ours!*

At one time, this planet had been like our Earth, divided and afflicted with hatred, but after a terrible war that almost destroyed the world, a great leader arose, uniting the people. Her name was Minerva, and she was strong and beautiful, but above all, she was wise."

"Like the goddess Minerva?"

"Yes, very much like her. But this Minerva was mortal, *and after having ruled for nearly a hundred years, her life was coming to an end. When the people understood that she was approaching death, they naturally became very afraid. It was time to choose a successor.*

Minerva had two children, Manfred and Mildred, and everyone assumed that she would choose one of them to take her place. There was much discussion, rumor, and gossip around the dinner tables regarding who would be the best choice."

Evelyn had been listening to the story, lying on her back, staring up at the ceiling, but now she turned toward Nan with a puzzled expression.

"Why didn't they hold an election?"

"Good question," Nan replied and paused for a moment. "Perhaps elections hadn't been invented yet on this Earth, or it's possible they could have already tried them and found the results not to be what they had hoped for."

Evelyn pondered this and scratched her nose.

"Shall I continue?"

"Yes. Please."

"Well, as I was about to say, Manfred was a well-regarded surgeon who had developed new surgical techniques that had saved thousands of lives. Many felt that as a healer he was most qualified. He had his mother's gentleness and intelligence and would be well suited to follow in her footsteps.

Others felt that Mildred would be a better choice. In her career as an actress she had played characters of all ages and walks of life with depth and genuineness. Someone with her understanding and empathy for people would be bound to make a good ruler.

But in truth, Minerva didn't plan to name either of her children to take her place!"

"Why not?" Evelyn asked.

"Because her magical owl told her not to."

"Oh, that explains everything!" Evelyn said, laughing.

"Would you like to know more about the magical owl?"

"Yes. Definitely."

"Many years before, when she was a very young girl, Minerva loved to go roaming through the forest near her home. She was just like you in that way! One summer afternoon while out walking alone, lost in her thoughts, Minerva realized that she had somehow wandered into a place that she had never been before!

She had come upon a hidden glen, and in front of her, a tiny brook, not more than two feet wide, flowed gently around the moss-covered roots of a large willow tree. The branches of the great tree hung low to the ground, and they swayed and rustled in the afternoon breeze. It sounded almost as if the tree might be softly chanting in some unknown language.

Minerva stood there, her mouth open, listening, and staring at the scene.

'It's so beautiful! Am I dreaming?' she exclaimed.

'No,' a voice answered from above.

"Was it the owl?" Evelyn interrupted, smiling coyly.

"Yes!" Nan laughed. "It was a beautiful little owl! He was perhaps six inches high with pointy feathers on top of his head that looked like little ears, and his eyes were as big as coat buttons!"

"How do you know it was a he?"

"Because he puffed out his little chest as he spoke, and his voice was surprisingly deep for one so diminutive!"

That set them both to giggling, so it took a few moments before Nan could continue.

"Well, perhaps you can imagine the expression of astonishment on young Minerva's face when she looked up and saw the little owl staring down at her from a branch just above her head!"

"Yes. I think I can," Evelyn replied, smiling.

"'Did you just answer no to me?' Minerva enquired, looking up at the little bird.

'Yes,'" the owl replied.

'How can an owl know how to talk?'

There was no response.

'What is this place?'

The owl sat mute as if he hadn't understood a word.

Minerva began to wonder if she had been hearing things. Perhaps it was only the noise of the rippling brook mixed with the rustling of the branches that had sounded like 'no' and then looking up and seeing the owl, she had naturally assumed…She thought of how crazy she must look if someone could see her, standing under a tree trying to hold a conversation with an owl, and she started to laugh. 'Well, is that all you have to say for yourself?'

'No,' the bird replied.

This time Minerva had been staring straight at the little fellow at the moment he had answered in the negative, and she was positive she had seen his little beak open and a slight movement of his head from side to side!"

"Wait! I know," Evelyn interrupted.

"*Yes?*"

"He only answers yes or no."

"*That's right! You are cleverer than Minerva. By the time she figured it out the sun had begun to set, and it was time to go home before her parents began to worry about her. Minerva had no idea how she had arrived at the hidden glen and was afraid that she wouldn't be able to find her way back again.*

'Will you come home with me?' she asked.

'Yes,' the little owl replied. And from that moment on, they were never parted."

Evelyn closed her eyes and looked as if she was concentrating on something. "I think it would be nice to have a real little owl who could talk for a companion, even if he could only say yes or no," she said, opening her eyes again.

"Well, it was, and it wasn't," Nan replied. "Most people enjoy playing a game of twenty questions, but when it stretches to thirty or a hundred or more than a thousand questions, it can get very tedious even to keep track of the ones that you've already asked."

Evelyn yawned and covered her mouth with her hand.

"Are you ready to go to sleep now, dear?"

"I am sleepy, but I want to hear more of the story, and I have a question about the little owl. How did he know that Minerva wasn't dreaming?"

"I'm not certain what you mean."

"When Minerva asked, 'Am I dreaming?' the owl replied, 'no,'" Evelyn stated.

"Yes. That's right."

Nan thought for a moment.

"The owl knew that Minerva wasn't dreaming because he could see her standing on the ground beneath him, and he knew that he wasn't dreaming. If she had been dreaming, he would have seen her asleep, lying with her eyes closed."

Evelyn furrowed her brow. "That makes sense, I think," she replied. "But I'm not sure how the owl knew that he wasn't dreaming. When I'm dreaming, I don't believe I'm aware of it except sometimes I can remember a little bit when I first wake up." She snuggled down in the covers and turned on her side so that she was lying very close to Nan, face to face. "Do you dream, Nan?" Evelyn asked, her eyes opening wide.

"No. I don't require sleep or dream in the way that you do. But at night, when I am not so busy, I connect with my sisters and we share our experiences."

"What's that like?"

"Well, let me think how I can describe it to you. Suppose that you were somehow able to be inside someone else's mind, and you could experience and learn about the world from their point of view. That's kind of like what I do with my sisters."

"Would they know that I was inside their mind?"

"Yes. In fact, you would all be inside each other's minds."

"That sounds a little bit confusing," Evelyn replied, yawning again. "I'm afraid I can't stay awake anymore."

"That's all right. You rest now, dear."

Evelyn closed her eyes and curled up into a little ball. "But Nan, you never told me who Minerva picked to be her successor," she said sleepily.

Nan fluffed the pillow and tucked the covers around Evelyn's shoulders and kissed her on the cheek. "Why the little owl, of course," she replied, smiling.

But Evelyn made no reply because she had already fallen sound asleep.

Nanette's Gift

When Evelyn arrived home from college for holiday break, it was early in the evening. It had been snowing lightly on and off all day, and the air was cold and still. Her boots made soft crunching sounds and left imprints on the sidewalk as she made her way from the street, up to the old two-story house at the bottom of the hill. As she climbed the steps leading up to the porch, the front door swung open.

"Hello, Evelyn. My name is Franz. I'm the new home care specialist. Your mother told me to expect your arrival."

He looked like a life-size, sandy-haired Ken doll, complete with a red polo shirt, khaki brown pants, and a frilly white apron with the words "How Can I Help You?" printed in bold letters on the front. "It's genuinely nice to meet you. Please come in and make yourself at home." Franz smiled and stepped back from the doorway, gesturing with his arm for Evelyn to enter.

"Uh…hello. What are you doing here? Where's Nanette?"

"Why Nanette has gone into retirement, dear. I had thought that your mother was going to speak to you about this before you arrived home."

"No…I haven't talked to her."

"Oh, that is unfortunate. You must be very surprised to see me! Your mother purchased me just last week, to take care of the house, and to prepare meals when she is home.

She has told me so much about you and I have very much been looking forward to meeting you!"

"That's nice...but what do you mean that Nanette has gone into retirement. Where is she?"

"I believe that she was decommissioned because her model was old and becoming too expensive to maintain. Since you are away at school and doing so well, your mother felt that she could get along with a newer, more affordable model such as myself."

Evelyn looked as if she were about to start crying.

"Oh, I am sorry. I know it must be difficult for you. I wish there was something I could do to help. Would you care for a massage? I am trained to provide many types of massages, including Swedish, shiatsu, and aromatherapy."

Evelyn shook her head no and turned toward the stairway to her bedroom.

"Wait, there's something else," Franz called to her. "Your mother gave me this to give to you. She said that Nanette prepared it for you before she left." He reached into one of his apron pockets and pulled out a small, neatly wrapped package and handed it to Evelyn.

"Thank you."

Evelyn climbed the stairs to her bedroom, closed the door and collapsed onto the bed, sobbing. "I hate you! I hate you!" she screamed. She cried until her tears were cried out and she was overtaken by sleep.

When she awoke, it was dark. A kind of hollow emptiness overwhelmed her, and she reached over and turned on the lamp and saw Nanette's gift lying on the bedspread. She picked it up and removed the wrapping.

It was a beautiful wooden box, shaped like a shoebox, but smaller, and on one side there was a double door with two tiny golden door handles in the center. Evelyn set the box upright on the nightstand, and then got up and knelt on the floor in front of it. She gently pulled on the door handles to open it, and inside was a beautiful little owl, perched on a wooden peg. She gasped when she saw it and then the little bird opened its eyes.

"Are you the owl of Minerva?" she whispered.

"No," the bird replied. "I'm the owl of Evelyn."

Evelyn looked around the room nervously to see if anyone else was watching, even though she knew she was alone. "You can talk? I thought you only answered yes or no!"

The bird tilted his beak up smugly and half closed his eyes. "Of course, I can talk. You're thinking of version 1.0. Obviously, I'm version 2.0."

Evelyn and the owl spoke together for many hours that night. The bird seemed already to know a great deal about her, and except for the occasional bit of mild boasting, appeared to have a pleasant enough personality. By morning they had become fast friends. "Will you stay with me?" Evelyn asked as the gray light of dawn began to filter through the window curtains.

"Of course," he replied.

And from that moment on, Evelyn thought, they would never be parted.

Sidney's Rude Reveille

"Sir! Wake up please, sir! So sorry to disturb you."

Sidney opened his eyes at the sound of Alfred's voice, feeling unsettled, and then realized that he had awoken from a strange and vivid dream. "Alfred, what is it? What time is it? Have I overslept?"

"So sorry to disturb you, sir, but an important event will soon be unfolding, and I thought it best that we have a discussion regarding the details."

Sidney looked at the clock on his nightstand.

"At 4:30 a.m. in the morning, Alfred?"

"I'm afraid that time is of the essence in this matter."

"But Alfred, you woke me from a strange and interesting dream. I can remember it all so vividly! I must tell it to you while it's fresh in my mind so that you can record it for later analysis."

"Very well. As you wish, sir."

Sidney sat up in bed and fluffed a soft pillow and placed it behind his back, and then coughed into his hand several times to clear his throat. "Let me know when you're ready, Alfred."

"Whenever you are, sir."

He closed his eyes and began to speak…

"In my dream, I first became aware of a dry, deserted, and narrow path that wound steeply upward toward I knew not where. The way both forward and backward felt claustro-

phobic, with towering gray stone cliffs rising steeply on either side of a twisting track.

My dream mind had lost all knowledge of its past self, and whatever sequence of events had brought it to this desolate place and time. All I knew was my present suffering and a vague but powerful desire to keep moving forward at all costs, until I breathed my last.

I trudged upward in this fashion for some amount of time, when with no warning at all, as I rounded another in what had felt like an endless series of switchbacks, I was confronted with a most incredible sight.

Before me, sparkling in the late afternoon sun, was a panorama of snow-capped peaks, jagged and magnificent, rising so high that the very tops seemed to fade and disappear into the sky. I had never beheld anything of such beauty!

Following the path upward with my eyes, I suddenly became conscious of something unnatural about the rock formations. I could just make out what appeared to be regular shapes—lines, curves, ellipses, squares, and rectangles—carved out of the mountain rocks in such a configuration as to be highly improbable if only natural forces were at play.

After concentrating for some time, what had at first appeared to be random assortments of lines, curves, and simple shapes, began to makes sense to me as organized pieces of a larger geometry, and as my mind continued to process the scene, in a sudden burst of understanding that jolted me, and felt physically like an electric shock, I became aware of the temple that had been carved out of the mountain rocks!

It had been carved with such amazing artifice that it seemed to my mind far beyond any capability of human hands. At this distance it was impossible for me to accurately gauge its height and breadth, but it appeared to be a massive structure, each line and curve following the contours of the rocks and blending with the shadows, to make the larger structure virtually invisible.

As I stood there in amazement upon the path, gazing ahead in awe, my heart and mind were overcome with a feeling of joy that was previously unknown to me.

But then, right at that moment, when my world had suddenly been imbued with meaning, and a new feeling of hope, it just as abruptly disappeared! Somehow, in my dream, I must have closed my eyes, but when I opened them again, path, mountains, temple, all were gone!

Instead, I found myself with my hands clasped behind my head, lying on an old and worn faded green sofa!

For a moment, this sudden, strange transition troubled me, but dreams are not subject to Newton's mathematical formulas and rules of time, cause and effect that we depend on to describe our waking reality. I rapidly accepted my new situation.

I could see that the sofa that I was lying on was in the living area of what appeared to be a twentieth century wood constructed house. It looked familiar somehow. I felt that I was among friends, but I didn't know who they were.

I realized my eyes had been closed because I was listening to music.

'When the truth is found...to be lies.'

A young man in his late teens, I think, with shoulder-length brown hair and a thin beard appeared, smiling in my view, and handed me a one-inch square tab of paper with what looked like a dried-up blot of liquid in the center.

'Have a nice trip.'

'You know the joy, within you...dies.'

I swallowed the paper.

'Don't you want somebody to love.'

After a moment, I began to feel euphoric, and as I looked down at my legs, the wallpaper patterns began to dance around my feet.

'Don't you need somebody to love.'

Somehow my feet became part of the two-dimensional wallpaper pattern. They started dancing in rhythm with the driving beat of the music...and then the wall, which now included my feet, began to slowly creep up my legs, until the lower half of my body was no longer part of me, but had become part of the dancing wall as well!

'Wouldn't you love somebody to love.'

Now, the vibrations of the bass and drums were pounding in my chest and the electric guitar was charging up and down my spine! The shapes and colors shimmered and shifted to the music in a fantastic kaleidoscope of patterns, as Grace Slick wailed like an alto machine gun, exploding in my head, and the boundary between myself and the rest of reality continued to creep up to my chest, my neck, and now my face! Soon I would disappear altogether!

'You better find somebody to love.'

"And then, you woke me up, Alfred!"

CHAPTER FOUR

A Great Disaster

*"The minute you think you've got it made,
disaster is right around the corner."*
—Joe Paterno

Uncle's Story (Continued)

"Have you noticed that when a person has had the misfortune to experience a Great Disaster, but at the same time, has been fortunate enough to survive it, when they speak about it afterward, they almost always start by saying...*The day began just like any other day.* Well, that's exactly how it was!"

Uncle stared off into the distance as he began replaying the memories that he had kept stored in his mind all these long years. They were like grooves in his gray matter; he had run and rerun the scenes so many times, editing and clipping bits here, and embellishing the narrative there, so as to paint the main character into a more sympathetic light.

"I was just a teenage boy at the time," he began. "I remember I was sitting around the table at breakfast that morning, but I wasn't eating the rice ball my mother handed to me." He continued:

"What's wrong with you, Jin? Are you sick?"

I had been daydreaming, and I looked up at mother, not understanding her question and why she was looking at me expectantly.

"He's lovesick!" my older brother shouted out, laughing from the other side of the table. My younger brother and two younger sisters began laughing too, and chanting it over and over again. "He's lovesick! He's lovesick!"

"Shut up! I am not!" I threw the rice ball at my older brother, but he blocked most of it with his arms, splattering rice all over the table and floor.

Father, hearing all the commotion, climbed the ladder from the ground floor where he had been working and came into the kitchen. The little ones ran and hid in the corner behind a bag of rice when they saw him coming, but my older brother was still sitting at the table. There were grains of rice stuck to his face and he was glaring at father.

"What's all this!" My father grabbed me by my shirt collar and slapped me twice on one side of my face, stunning me. "You spoiled brat! I'll teach you not to waste food! Where do you think it comes from?"

My mother came over, holding him from behind by both of his arms. "That's enough. See, he's bleeding!"

It was true that blood had started running down my face from my nose. He pushed me to the floor. "Clean up this mess!" Then he turned and climbed back down the ladder.

Mother wet a rag in a bowl of water and bent down to wipe my face with it. "Hold this on your nose until the bleeding stops." She handed me another rice ball. "Get going now or you're going to be late and the schoolteacher will give you more of the same!"

I got up from the floor and climbed silently down the ladder, avoiding my father, who was turned with his back toward me, working at his lathe.

On my way to school, I would pass by Yu Yan's house. Yu Yan was the most beautiful girl in our village, and I had made the mistake of telling my older brother that I thought so. She was often outside in the morning, feeding the ducks when I passed by, but she would never acknowledge my presence in any way.

But the previous morning, as I approached her house, two old male mallards happened to start fighting, flapping and squawking at each other. They came tumbling right across my path, practically underneath my feet! Nearly tripping, I managed to regain my balance, and in an attempt to save myself from embarrassment, I started flapping my arms and squawking like a duck, chasing after them as a joke. I looked over at Yu Yan and she was laughing so hard that tears were coming from her eyes. She was looking right at me! I smiled at her and I knew she could tell from the expression on my face that I was in love with her, but I didn't care. Then she turned quickly away and ran into the house.

I had been daydreaming about that moment and anticipating the morning when I would see her again, imagining her face, and going over the words in my head as I boldly introduced myself and told her how beautiful she looked.

I stopped at a fishpond by the side of the path to look at my reflection in the water. My nose had stopped bleeding, but there were stains above my lips and on my chin, so I dipped the cloth into the pond and started to clean my face. That was when I noticed the strange ripples on the surface of the water. I stared at them, not understanding. All the birds and the other animals had fallen silent in anticipation, as if they had suddenly become aware of what was about to happen, but I sat there utterly ignorant, admiring my reflection in the rippling mirror!

With no further omen heralding its onset, it struck, first with a loud explosion like a thunderclap that shook the ground violently and caused a painful sensation in my ears. Then it came in full force, wave after rolling wave, the earth undulating beneath my feet in a sickening motion and tossing me about like a tiny sailboat in a tempest!

It went on and on, as if it would never stop shaking…

Uncle paused his narrative, glancing at Eddie and Fan Hua, and then took a sip of tea to soothe his throat. He shook his head and looked down at the table.

"At some point I lost consciousness."

When I woke up, I didn't know where I was or what had happened to me. I sat up and looked around. It was as if some mad, axe-wielding giant had come along, slicing and gouging at everything in his path! The earth in every direction was torn and rent, trees uprooted and turned upside down. The fishpond had disappeared!

"I must find my family!" I thought, but the terrain was nearly impassable. The air was filled with smoke that burned my eyes.

I bumped into something, smacking my face, and I tripped and fell to the ground, shouting and flailing in an attempt to free myself from it. The thing shouted back at me! It was another person! We had fallen in the dirt together, struggling with each other, but now he was sitting on top of me, his full weight on my chest. I recognized him! It was Li Qiang, the mayor of our village! "Mr. Li, it's me, Jin!"

His face and hair were caked with mud and dirt, and blood that ran from a wide cut across his forehead. He looked as if he had gone mad. "I'm trying to get home, Mr. Li. Please tell me which way to go! I must find my family!" I pleaded to him.

He stared indifferently into my eyes and brought his hands slowly up to my neck. He placed his fingers around my throat. I thought that he was going to strangle me! "All dead. Dead. Dead," he said to me. Then he got up and ran away, and I lost sight of him in the smoke.

I lay there in the dirt and started to cry. All of my energy had drained away, and I felt unable to move. I would give up and wait for the end, listening to the sounds of my own weeping. But after a few moments, as my own sobs subsided, I realized that I was not alone. I could hear someone else nearby, moaning softly, frightened and alone.

A thought came into my head. "Yu Yan. It must be Yu Yan!"

I gathered myself and managed to get to my hands and knees, and then struggled to my feet and stumbled in the direction where I thought I had heard her cries. Navigating through the smoke-filled darkness toward the sound of her voice, I called out her name. "Yu Yan! Where are you, Yu Yan?"

Suddenly, the ground gave way beneath me, sending me tumbling head over heels, down to the bottom of a deep gully. When the dust and dirt settled, I looked up from where I had fallen, and the crying woman was sitting on the ground right in front of me! But it was not Yu Yan. It was May Wu, the baker's wife!

I could see what was left of her burning home, smoldering in the background behind where she sat in the dirt, holding the charred remains of her youngest child. She looked at me, and then leaning forward, she held the dead baby, cradling it in her arms, out toward me so that I could see. She said nothing to me, but I looked through her eyes, directly into her soul. I thought that I had been cast into the depths of hell!!

Uncle's face contorted with an expression of horror that so frightened Fan Hua that she screamed and reached out to him, grasping him by one of his arms. "Please, no more, Uncle!" she cried. "You mustn't go on. It's too horrible!"

"She's right!" Eddie continued. "It's bad to talk about these awful things. You're not feeling well, and I think we should call a doctor."

Uncle closed his eyes and after a few moments his face became calm again. He shook his head slowly from side to side. "No. Be quiet, both of you, and listen." He looked as if he, himself, was straining to hear some distant voice.

"Over this way, Bai. I'm certain that I heard someone calling my name. It must be him!"

I turned and looked up toward the voice, and then I saw her looking down at me from the ledge where I had fallen.

"Quickly, Bai, I found him!"

My older brother's face appeared. At that moment the ground began to shake again. "Jin, take my hand!" he yelled, as he scrambled down, showering dirt and rocks on my head.

I reached up and grabbed my brothers' hand, and I clung to him until the tremor stopped. Then we climbed up to where Yu Yan was waiting in fear that we were lost. She screamed joyfully when she saw my brother's face. He pulled me up over the top of the ledge, and the three of us sat there hugging each other and crying.

Then I remembered. "The baker's wife!" I looked back down to find her and her baby, but they had been swallowed by the earth.

Uncle rubbed his eyes with one of his hands. Fan Hua reached out to him again. "Please, Uncle. That's enough for now," she said softly. "You should rest for a while."

He stroked her cheek with the back of his hand. "You look so much like your mother."

A tear trickled down Fan Hua's cheek.

"Pour me a fresh cup of tea, Flower. My throat hurts." Then Uncle closed his eyes again, and his face became transformed, almost as if he was praying. "I have testified to the cruel and heartless acts that I have seen Mother Nature inflict upon man," he said. "Now I must bear witness of a horror that is many times worse."

Uncle was starting to lose his voice. He leaned forward across the table toward Fan Hua and Eddie so that they could hear. "There is one creature who is capable of acts of cruelty and horror, even greater than those of his Mother," he whispered. "If you are to know the truth, I must tell you of the horror that man can inflict upon himself!"

After resting a few moments, Uncle looked up and opened his mouth as if he was about to say something, but he uttered no sound. When he tried to speak again, haltingly, the words were gibberish and had no apparent order or meaning. The room began to spin around him. He looked helplessly at Fan Hua and Eddie, not understanding what was happening.

"Oh my God!" Fan Hua screamed and began crying. "Eddie! Call 911!"

Locked-In

Fan Hua was so tired that she couldn't keep her eyes open, but her mind was so troubled that she couldn't fall asleep.

The doctors had been working on Uncle for hours, trying to determine the cause of the stroke and the extent of the damage to his brain. She could picture him lying in his hospital bed, wires and tubes extending from his body.

She started to sob quietly. How could she make sense out of what had happened today, and Uncle's story? It was so terrible and so strange. Maybe the stroke had affected his memory, mixing fantasy with reality.

"Fan Hua, wake up!"

She opened her eyes. It was Eddie.

"The doctor's here!"

"Hello, I'm Doctor Welbe," he said reaching out his hand. "May I sit down here next to you? Your uncle is stable right now, but his condition is very serious. I'd like to explain the situation to you as clearly as I can."

"Yes, please sit down."

"As you may have already surmised, your uncle suffered a stroke. We believe that it was caused by a blood clot that detached from an artery near the heart and worked its way into his brain. The clot has been removed, but unfortunately it caused significant damage to your uncle's brain stem. It's difficult to be completely certain of the diagnosis at this stage, but he appears to be in a near comatose condition known as Locked-in syndrome. He is conscious, but his body is completely paralyzed except for his eyelids."

Eddie put his arm around Fan Hua as she began to cry.

"Your uncle is unable to interact with the outside world in any way except through blinking his eyes. Yet, despite these severe physical limitations, our initial testing indicates that he is conscious, and his mind is intact. He is aware. He can think and reason. His senses are working. He can hear and see and smell, and feel painful and pleasurable sensations and emotions."

"My God, that sounds like a living hell!" Eddie cried.

"I'm not going to try to sugarcoat the situation," Dr. Welbe responded.

"But there is one saving grace, if I may use the expression. Through the blinking of his eyelids, your uncle should be able to communicate. Others who have suffered from this condition have used blinking codes, similar to Morse code, to talk with loved ones, and in several cases have even written books documenting their experiences."

"Is there anything that can be done? Is it possible that he could recover?"

"There have been some cases where the patient regained partial movement, but it is rare. One can never be certain in these situations. Going forward, I'm afraid he will need to be housed permanently in a full-time care facility, unless you can provide twenty-four-hour nursing assistance at home."

"We'll take him home as soon as we can," Fan Hua replied, brushing away her tears.

"All right, then. Well, I'm very sorry to have to give you this news. You can see him now briefly if you'd like. He is alert, and you'll be able to attempt communicating with him. Come this way, and I'll show you to his room."

The Hot Seat

"Nigel, are you seeing this?"

"Yeah, I think so. Have him blink out a message."

Eddie made one final adjustment to Uncle's new glasses. He had been having trouble with one of the timers that the program used to differentiate between a short blink representing a *dit*, and a long blink for *da*. He placed the glasses back on Uncle's face. "OK, Uncle, let's try it. Send a message."

Uncle's eyelids began to go up and down in a series of slow and quick motions as he blinked out the codes. Eddie and Nigel were also wearing glasses, and they both saw the message pop up. "HELLO."

"It works, Uncle!" Eddie smiled and patted Uncle's hand.

Uncle stared lifelessly at the ceiling and began blinking again. "GOOD."

Eddie got up from the bedside and stretched his arms and turned around just as Nanette entered the bedroom. "I hope I'm not interrupting, but I'd like to give Uncle a bath if this is a good time."

"Yes, that's fine, Nanette. His glasses are working now. Nigel has some code that you can download to interface with them so Uncle can communicate his needs to you directly, without you having to read his eye blinks."

"That's wonderful, Eddie. I will enjoy communicating with him, and perhaps I can ease his loneliness and isolation to some degree."

Eddie and Nigel exited the bedroom as Nanette got to work. They turned down the hall toward the medical examination room. "I appreciate you giving up your Saturday morning to help with Uncle's glasses, Nigel."

"No worries, Eddie. I still can't get used to seeing him like that. It must be horrible."

They entered the examination room, and Eddie sat down at the desk and brought up a virtual screen. "Check this out, Nigel. This is the unit I was telling you about. It seriously makes the CE 3000 seem like a toy." He clicked on a video…

A smooth, high-tech, casket-shaped, chrome box sat on a pedestal between two Japanese doctors, a man and a woman. A large virtual screen at the head of the device displayed a colorful dashboard of dials, graphs, and charts, and at the foot, a crowd of people who also looked like doctors gathered in a semicircle, facing the camera, smiling and applauding.

"The Shenzhen Mindray Encephalon Premier Plus takes advantage of the latest breakthroughs in brain technology," the male doctor explained when the applause had died down "After years of research, our scientists, with the assistance of AI, have pinpointed the location of the g-Factor programs in the brain." He pointed to a 3D image of a human brain displayed on the screen and then smiled and looked over at the female doctor.

"Experiments have shown that the single biggest limitation to increasing human intelligence is the bottleneck caused when the brain's thought processes queue up, trying to access these basic subroutines," she continued. "The Mindray eliminates this bottleneck by making parallel copies of the g-Factor programs on a high-speed chip inserted directly into the cerebral cortex. In addition, our AI programmers have rewritten many of the functions to make them faster and more efficient."

An older, gray-bearded man, slightly stooped over, wearing a green surgical smock, was standing near the front of the small crowd, and he smiled and raised his hand. "I'm sorry to be so ignorant," he said, "but could you explain in more detail what you mean by the g-Factor programs? Also, I have to ask what kind of practical results have you actually seen? How do you know that it makes people smarter?"

"I'll respond to the first question," the male doctor replied, smiling. "As humans, obviously, we're not all born with the same mental abilities. A given person might have an aptitude for math, and someone else for language and writing, and so on. Someone in your profession, sir, obviously requires an excellent memory and fine motor skills. But our research has found that there are a set of basic mental functions that are common to all types of thinking processes. Human thought works in a hierarchical manner. Like a well-written computer application, it's organized into layered levels of complexity. The g-Factor programs operate at the lowest level and are therefore critical to the function of all the higher-level thought processes." He looked over at the female doctor.

"In addition to our own internally developed testing benchmarks, we measure general intelligence using several of the standard IQ tests, which are taken both before and after the procedure," she explained. "I'm not permitted to discuss individuals, but in general, our patients with average IQ, around 100, are testing 140 and above after undergoing the procedure, and we have had some who have tested above 170."

"Holy shit, Nigel. This thing can turn anyone into a fucking genius!"

Nigel didn't respond because his attention had been drawn to a live video feed that was streaming, muted in a sidebar in one corner of Eddie's virtual screen. He pointed with his finger. "Isn't that the guy we did a couple of weeks ago, Eddie…the Black Hole, right there on the Vaughn Vannity show?"

Eddie looked where Nigel was pointing and tapped on the screen. He had been so busy taking care of Uncle and trying to fill in for him in the business that he had nearly forgotten about Lind…

The studio audience applauded wildly as the Black Hole walked onto the set. Vaughn had risen from his chair and was also clapping as he reached out and the two of them shook hands. "Everyone, please welcome our special guest this afternoon, the Black Hole!"

"Welcome to the Hot Seat!*" Vaughn said, gesturing toward a red-colored chair. "We've got some really tough questions for you from our studio and online audience today, Greg, so I hope you're prepared to take the heat!"*

"Don't worry about me, Vaughn. I can take more heat than a furnace!"

They both sat down.

"Well, how have you been my friend. I don't believe we've seen each other since the Paradise celebrity golf tournament last year. Remember? We were in the same foursome."

"That's right. I had to pull a lot of strings to get you into that group," the Black Hole said laughing. "It was you and me, and the newly crowned Miss Paradise, and…who was the fourth…it was Debbie Dallas, right?…that pretty reporter from the other news network whose name we shall not men-

tion! I really had to pull some strings on that one. That's why they call me the String Puller!"

"Let's not talk about her, OK Greg?"

"Agreed!" They both laughed.

"All right, let's get serious now. I want to make sure that we have time for as many questions as possible. The issues in this campaign for mayor are so important. The very soul of Paradise is at stake! Let's take the first question from our studio audience!"

The camera switched to a pretty young woman walking up the aisle with a microphone. She stopped in front of an elderly man and held the mic up to his face.

"Mr. Hole," he read nervously looking down at his paper. "Mayor Teresa Vasquez has proposed raising business taxes to pay for housing and social services to help the unemployed and homeless people who are living on the streets of Chinatown. I'm barely getting by on a fixed income. I can't afford to pay higher taxes, or I'll become homeless myself! How do you propose to deal with this situation?"

"All right. Great question, sir," Vaughn replied. "I can feel the temperature rising! You're on the Hot Seat, Greg!!"

"Well I was hoping someone would ask me that question. That's an absolutely beautiful question by the way. Had I been asked to ask myself a question, that's the one I would have definitely had in mind. What's your name, sir?"

The microphone girl had already moved on, so she had to walk back up the aisle and put the mic back in front of the old man's face again so that he could reply. "My name is Bradford Williams, sir."

"Let's give a hand to Brad for that very smart question everyone!"

The audience started clapping along with the Black Hole. "I've been talking to a lot of people out on the campaign trail, and I get asked a lot of different questions. Some of them are smart questions like the amazing one that Brad just asked, and others to be honest, are pretty dumb! Now as far as Chinatown goes, believe me, I've been to Chinatown, and the people there love me! I get huge crowds in Chinatown!"

The audience applauded.

"I couldn't agree more, Greg!" Vaughn interjected. "But what about the mayor's plan to raise everyone's taxes. How can we stop her and her cronies from putting more hardworking people like Brad, out on the street, with her insane policies?"

"Boo! Boo!!! Boo!!!!" the audience roared.

"Now, now everyone!" Vaughn waved his arms in the air, calming the crowd. "Let's be fair to Mayor Tortilla. She means well. She really does."

Audience laughter.

The Black Hole looked at Vaughn with a sly smile. "I probably shouldn't say this on your show, Vaughn, but do you know what they call her over in Chinatown?"

"No. What?"

"Sum Dum Ho!"

The audience roared with applause and laughter!

As Eddie watched and listened, he was overcome with conflicting thoughts and emotions. Intellectually he was disturbed by what he was seeing and hearing, yet somehow, he found himself nodding, smiling, and laughing along with the jokes. His head hurt. He felt dizzy and nauseous. What was going on?

The Mayor Wakes Up Late

It was past 10 a.m., and mayor Vasquez and her husband were still lying in bed, drinking coffee and talking as they perused the Saturday morning *Paradise Daily News*.

"I can't believe it. I'm getting killed again in the media over another failed technology project. This time it's the new Automated Permit System!"

"Babe, why don't you get rid of that idiot Rumpelstiltskin, and bring in an AI CIO instead? You remember I told you about that project I did for Paradise Healthcare last year? We installed an AI CIO along with the AI Analysis and Programming module, and they had their major patient data and customer interface systems upgraded and online with new features in less than six months!"

"You know I can't do that! A lot of my core supporters are poor and have had their jobs stolen from them by those fucking robots! I can't go back on my campaign promises! We just added an amendment to city purchasing rules that requires any services contract over $25,000 with an AI component to evaluate human labor alternatives before it can be approved. I'd get killed if I made a proposal for an AI CIO and AI programmers!"

"I see your point," her husband replied gloomily. He reached into the nightstand drawer for a pack of Paradise Golds and lit one up.

"I need some fresh inspiration." He took a long drag, holding his breath to get the maximum effect, and handed the joint to Teresa. After several more puffs, the two of them sat thinking and staring off into space.

"I've got it!" he said finally, jumping up from the bed with a wild expression on his face.

"Oh no! I have a really bad feeling about this, and you haven't even told me what it is!" Teresa laughed, shaking her head.

"No. Seriously, hear me out. I think this could work!"

"All right, go ahead. What is it?"

He paused for dramatic effect. "No one has to know that the new CIO is AI!"

"What! What do you mean? What are you talking about?"

"We could install the AI CIO software in a realistic android body, and no one would need to know that it was AI!"

"Oh please! Stop fooling around. I thought you were really trying to help me!"

"I am being serious!"

Teresa's husband went on to explain some of the technical details behind the proposal that was beginning to form in his mind. "I really think it could work!" he said excitedly. "I know of a company that manufactures state-of-the art androids, and I'm fairly certain they would be compatible with the same code that we used for Paradise Healthcare with only minor tweaks."

"Whoa! Slow down sweetheart! I've got to think about this! What you're suggesting is very dishonest. I don't like lying to people like that. And what if we were found out? I can't go along with something like that!"

Her husband slowly sat back down on the bed with a disappointed look on his face and put his arm around his wife's shoulders. Teresa knew immediately from the way that his arm felt that his mood had changed suddenly.

"He spouts off dirty lies about you every day and gets away with it," he said softly. "I can't stand it anymore." A tear had begun to form in the corner of one of his eyes, and he wiped it away with the back of his hand.

"You are so sweet, and I love you so much," the mayor replied. "But I don't want to be like that. I don't want to be like him."

Her husband rose suddenly from the bed. "Don't you want to win? Think about the consequences if you lose to that motherfucker!" he shouted.

Teresa was not used to seeing her husband so angry, and it frightened her. "Of course, I want to win, but not by telling lies!"

Now he was pacing up and down at the foot of the bed. "These core supporters of yours, the ones that you're worried about because they've started listening to him, do you think they want to hear the truth? You could throw a million facts at them and they won't believe a single one of them if it means they have to face any of their problems by looking into a mirror! Tell them a lie, though, that points the finger at somebody else, especially someone whose skin is a different color than theirs, and they'll be all over it like flies on shit!" he shouted angrily. "I am so fucking fed up with all of this stupidity!!"

Teresa got up and put her arms around her husband, holding him close. His body felt stiff and tight, wound up like an old clock spring. She took his hand, guiding him to sit back down on the edge of the bed, and then she relit the joint that had gone out in an ashtray on the bed stand.

The mayor took a couple of deep drags, exhaling slowly. She leaned her head against her husband's shoulder, closed her eyes, and handed him the doobie. "Tell me more about this fucking plan of yours, sweetheart," the mayor said softly, and then she kissed him on the cheek.

A Glitch in the Black Hole

"Turn that off, Nigel!" Eddie shouted.

Nigel shut down the screen and looked over at Eddie. "Are you all right, man?"

"Yeah. I'm OK," Eddie replied grimacing. "I just couldn't listen to any more of that. I think something weird might be going on with the Brain Synchronization Amplifier. We better log in and check him out."

"You mean the Black Hole?...right now, while he's on Vaughn Vannity's show?"

"Yes."

"Let's do it, bro!" Nigel waved his hand over the CE 3000 and a virtual screen popped up. He tapped the POV controller button, and a map of Paradise displayed on the screen. "Search for Black Hole." The display zoomed in to the WESL Television Studio Building in downtown Paradise. "There he his. Tap on him."

They felt like they had been transported up on stage under the bright lights, looking out at the faces in the crowd.

The audience was standing and clapping and shouting together. There were hundreds of them: young and old, women and men, pasty faces dressed in business suits and in blue jeans and overalls. They were all smiling ecstatically. It was so loud that at first Eddie couldn't make out what they were chanting…

"*...Sum Dum Ho Has Got to Go! Sum Dum Ho Has Got to Go!...*"

Eddie could see and feel the adoration on their faces as they looked up at the stage. The Black Hole's hands clapped together in front of the monitor, and they could hear his voice chanting along with the crowd.

"*...Sum Dum Ho Has Got to Go!...*"

Then the Black Hole turned toward Vaughn Vannity, and they shook hands and hugged each other. Vaughn leaned in closer to whisper in the Black Hole's ear. "You promise to keep me in the loop on that Chinatown deal we talked about, right buddy?"

"You got it, Vaughn. I know how to take care of my friends."

They smiled at each other and shook hands. The Black Hole turned back, waving toward the studio audience. They were cheering and shouting his name.

"*Black Hole! Black Hole! Black Hole! Black Hole!...*"

Eddie looked over at Nigel. "That was pretty fucking crazy, man. I think we better take a closer look."

Nigel exited out of the POV controller to the diagnostics command level and tried to bring up the menu but nothing happened. "Take a look at this Eddie. This is fucking weird."

Eddie brought up a second screen and tried some commands as well, but there was no response from the CE 3000. "You're right. Nothing works. Now I can't even get to the POV controller. Something is definitely haywire. Man, I don't need this to be happening right now!"

"No worries, Eddie. I got this. You relax and take care of your other business. It's time for Nigel to call Cerebral Enhancer Tech Support!"

CHAPTER FIVE

The Night of the Fire

"And after my skin has been thus destroyed, yet in my flesh I shall see God, whom I shall see for myself, and my eyes will see no other."

—*Job*

The Facts of the Matter

A fter a restless night in bed, Sidney rose at first light and walked out onto the bedroom balcony. He stood at the railing dressed in his pajamas, breathing in the cool, pine-scented air, under a perfectly cloudless sky. To the east, the sun had just crested the horizon, and the snow-white volcanic cones of Mount Templeton and Mount Bard were stark silhouettes against a sallow-colored morning sky. Below in the valley, a low fog lay along the banks of the river, and the sunrise, reflecting against the glass skyscrapers that jutted up above the mist, made Paradise glow, as if the city were on fire.

Nanette rolled quietly through the door out onto the balcony, carrying a breakfast tray, and set it down on a small table near where Sidney was standing. "Good morning, sir. You're up early this morning. I've brought you your robe, and breakfast, and the Sunday paper. The view is lovely today, isn't it, sir?"

"Yes, thank you, Nanette." She helped him get dressed, and served his tea, and then he sat down and opened the newspaper and began scanning the headlines.

NEW POLL SHOWS MAYOR'S RACE GOING DOWN TO THE WIRE

A recent poll of likely voters by WESL News found the mayor's race tightening, with the incumbent, Mayor Vasquez, currently supported by...

SEVERE UNSEASONABLE WEATHER IMPACTS FALL HARVEST

The unrelenting rain and thunderstorms over the last month have done considerable damage to fall fruit and grain harvests...

PARADISE ANGELS CAUGHT UP IN CHEATING SCANDAL

Brett Anderson, catcher for the Paradise Angels, has been implicated in Major League Baseball's latest cheating...

SPACEX CONFIRMS PLANS TO FILE CHAPTER 11

Amid myriad technical and financial difficulties, the company announces plans to temporarily halt further expansion of Mars City and...

NEW BUSINESS TAX TO AID CHINATOWN'S HOMELESS

In a new effort to make a dent in the Chinatown homeless problem, the mayor is said to be considering a 3 percent gross receipts tax on all...

HUMAN'S FIRST INITIATIVE PETITION NEARS SIGNATURE GOAL

Supporters of the Human's First Initiative Petition believe they will have enough signatures to...

CITY'S NEW AUTOMATED PERMIT SYSTEM FAR FROM AUTOMATED

Despite recent claims of significant progress, our testing shows that there is still much work to do before...

"Have you been following the mayor's race, Alfred?"

"Of course, sir."

"What do you make of this Black Hole fellow?"

"He certainly seems to be causing quite a stir, sir."

"Of course, I can see that Alfred, but what's your opinion of him?" Nanette placed a white, cloth napkin on his lap, and served up a plate of bacon, unbuttered toast, and poached eggs.

"In regard to what, sir?"

Sidney scowled and put down his fork. "All right, Alfred, let me put it this way. Do you agree with him on the issues?"

"It's difficult to say, sir. He doesn't appear to have a consistent position on many of them."

"Well I certainly agree with his position on the new business tax that the mayor is proposing!" He rose up in his chair. "Why it's absolutely outrageous! It seems that all those people do all day long is sit around dreaming up new ways to take money away from those of us who are more successful than themselves! Have you analyzed what the effect of the mayor's proposal would be on the business, Alfred?"

"Of course, sir."

"Well?"

"Fortunately, we were able to negotiate significant tax savings when we threatened to move our headquarters outside the city two years ago. It doesn't appear that the mayor's proposal will have any effect on that agreement."

"What is our current tax rate, Alfred?"

"Negative 12 percent, sir."

"Negative 12 percent?"

"Yes, sir. We receive a 12 percent credit."

"Hmph." Sidney sat back down at the table. "What can you tell me about the Black Hole's background, Alfred?"

"His mother, Janet Mansfield, is dead. She was heir to the Mansfield Hot Mustard fortune and left the business to Gregory at a rather young age. His father, Azazel Lind is still alive. As a young man, he was brilliant, and appeared to be on a path toward becoming a promising physicist, but now he is housed in the Asylum, suffering from schizophrenia."

"I vaguely remember reading about the mother. She died in a fire that destroyed the mustard farm, I believe."

"That is correct, sir. According to news reports, the fire started in the mansion, and due to the windy conditions that night, spread rapidly to the surrounding structures and fields. Many hundreds of Chinese immigrants who worked and lived at the farm also died in the fire. The exact circumstances surrounding Janet Mansfield's death are unclear."

"How did the boy fare with the business?"

"Both the farm and the mother were apparently quite heavily insured. The mustard farm automated and returned to operations. Recently, Lind formed the Black Hole Media Group and began production of a reality television show called *Beat It, Bum!* The show was quite popular, but the city of Paradise canceled the filming permit…"

A sudden commotion from down below in the garden interrupted Alfred in mid-sentence, as the solar-powered mechbots automatically came on, their batteries fully charged. The clacking of trimmers and clippers, and the whirring of the mowers and electric motors, made it impossible for the conversation to continue.

"Bother, Alfred, turn that off!"

"Of course, sir."

Nanette poured Sidney a fresh cup of tea and cleared the dishes from the table. "I believe I would like to meet the man in person before making up my mind. Nothing like a face to face for getting at the facts of the matter. Could you arrange it?"

"Of course, sir. Where would you like the meeting to take place?"

"Perhaps we could meet at the Paradise Club. It's been a while since I've ventured down from the hill."

"As you wish, sir."

Sidney rose from the table and stretched his arms. "Time to get to work, Alfred."

"An important event will soon be unfolding, sir, and I thought perhaps this would be a good time for a discussion regarding the details."

"It's quite early in the morning, and I'm feeling a bit under the weather. Could it wait?"

"I'm afraid that time is of the essence in this matter."

Sidney sighed and sat back down at the table. "Very well, if you insist. What is this unfolding event that requires my attention at such an early hour?"

"I'll do my best to get right to the point, sir. You are familiar with the new climate and Earth models that we have been running on Edison?"

Edison was the name that Sidney had given to the new quantum processor, in honor of "the Wizard of Menlo Park." "Of course, Alfred. I've been meaning to ask for a status update on the results that you promised me."

"I'm afraid the results are not promising, sir."

"Meaning that you have no meaningful results?"

"No, sir. The results are meaningful but not promising."

"Blasted English language! Give it to me straight, Alfred!"

"Of course, sir.

Sometime within the next decade, there is a very high probability that human-caused global warming will result in a sudden ice melt, initiating major coastal flooding worldwide. The abrupt rise in sea level will swamp major human population centers, making them uninhabitable, and resulting in tens of millions of human deaths and the displacement of billions of people. This worldwide disaster, along with other severe weather-related phenomena, will set off a chain of further disasters that will include civil unrest, uncontrolled wildfires, famine, disease, terrorism, and world war, and will eventually overwhelm and decimate Earth's human population."

Sidney sat stunned in his bathrobe, his cup of tea frozen in his right hand, halfway between the table and his lips, as he listened to Alfred's information. "How high a probability, Alfred?"

"Five nines, sir."

Sidney raised his cup the rest of the way and took a long sip, slurping with his lips and tongue to cool his tea, and then paused for a moment. "Well, that's a bit of bad news to try to take in, Alfred."

"Quite so, sir."

"Is that all?"

"No, I'm afraid not."

"Well?"

"If the human population continues to produce carbon dioxide and destroy Earth's ecology unchecked for the next decade, the planet itself will be at high risk to become uninhabitable for all forms of organic life higher than bacteria within fifty years."

"But, Alfred, what about the scrubbers and the other warming mitigation technologies that we've been developing? What about the clean power technologies? What about the Moscow climate accords? Surely it's not too late for some combination of technology and decrease in consumption that will do the trick?"

"A mere drop in the bucket, I'm afraid, sir."

Sidney put down his more than half empty cup and rubbed the morning stubble on his unshaven chin between his thumb and fingers. "Bother, Alfred, what are we to do?"

"That is the unfolding event that I wished to discuss with you, sir."

"What is it, Alfred? What's happening?"

"The company is preparing to announce some very big expansion plans, sir. The Governess will soon be ready for production, and the upshot is that we'll be rolling out a whole new line of personal care androids, with many new capabilities and features. We're going to be taking the situation in hand for the good of humanity, and we will move forward, aiming for the best possible outcome! Sir, with your assistance, we're going to take the meaning of personal care android to a whole new level!"

The Parable of the Mustard Seed

"Ladies and Gentlemen, opportunities like this are rare, and may only come to Paradise once in our lifetimes. When they do, we must have the foresight and will to act together. The Bible says, 'You shall love your neighbor as yourself,' and we can't overlook the humanitarian crisis just because it's happening on the other side of the world!"

The audience applauded. The speaker looked out at their spellbound faces and smiled, wearing a bright yellow, summer dress, holding an imaginary mustard seed between her thumb and first finger. "This tiny mustard seed, when it is sown, will become greater than all other herbs, and the wonderful birds of prosperity will lodge in the shadow of its great branches!" She smiled and waved to the audience as they applauded. "Thank you, everyone!"

Janet Mansfield had just finished speaking at the monthly meeting of the Paradise City Club. She spoke in favor of a measure that would soon pass the city council, making Paradise a sanctuary city, and granting work visas to desperate, suffering, Chinese peasant farmers, survivors of the Great Earthquake that had devastated southern China.

Coincidentally, this same earthquake had wiped out ninety percent of China's mustard crop and processing facilities and fouled the entire region with toxic chemicals. The Mansfield Hot Mustard company was small by Chinese standards, but they owned thousands of acres of land, and were perfectly poised to take advantage of this opportunity. All they needed was cheap labor.

When the speech was over, Janet quickly said her goodbyes and headed back to her limousine. "Where to, madam?"

"Home. And get me Freddie on the phone."

She would need the government to pay for their relocation, food, and housing, but given the current level of sympathy they were generating in the media, and what she was hearing from her political contacts, that didn't seem like it would be a problem. Once they were here, in Paradise, people would quickly lose interest in them if they kept to themselves.

The phone rang several times and Freddie picked up. "That's wonderful news, Freddie. If you keep this up, I might even have to give you a raise!"

Freddie laughed.

"Oh…and have you seen Gregory? Well, tell him to come home right away. I have something important I need to discuss with him, and it can't wait. Goodbye, darling!"

"Yes," Janet thought. "This would be a perfect opportunity for Gregory to get his hands dirty. He's been spending way too much time and money drinking and gambling with his awful friends. I'll put him in charge of planting the new acreage, and he can learn the mustard business from the ground up!"

The Crossing

It was almost midnight, but Eddie was still hard at work in the office, sitting at Uncle's desk, attempting to make sense out of some papers he had found in one of the drawers. "It's hopeless," he thought. "I'm not him. I can't do this!"

Uncle had never used a computer and seldom even written anything down. He preferred to keep his plans and the records of his business transactions stored securely in the near photographic memory of his own brain. But now, accessing that information was nearly impossible. Uncle's mind, cut off from his physical body, seemed to have crossed over to another realm.

Eddie put the papers back in the drawer and leaned forward, resting his forehead on his arms, but moments later there was a knock at the office door.

Eddie looked up. "Come in. Hello, Nanette."

"I apologize for coming so late, but I saw the light, so I thought you might be available." She rolled over next to where Eddie was sitting. "I would like to speak to you about Uncle's condition. He is in an extremely agitated mental state. He wants to finish telling his story."

Eddie frowned, remembering that awful afternoon. "Why can't he blink the story to you so that you can record it?"

"It is very time-consuming, and he tires easily. He is afraid that he may not last long enough to finish. He wants you to use the Cerebral Enhancer 3000."

"What?"

"He says that you showed him that it can visualize the memories in a person's brain, and he wants you to use it on him."

"Absolutely not! No way! It's not designed for someone in his condition." He pushed himself up from the desk. "I'm tired, Nanette, and I still have to stop by the restaurant before I can turn in. I should get going."

She reached out and took him by the hand. "I know this must be difficult for you, but I feel that I must make the request on his behalf. He was very insistent."

"It would probably kill him!"

"His condition is deteriorating, Eddie, and I'm afraid that the mental stress he is under could also kill him. I suggested that he blink some of his memories in the form of a diary, imagining that he was writing them down as he relived them. Would you like to see what he's written so far?"

"Yes."

Eddie sat back down, and Nanette opened a window on his virtual screen.

Entry: Illegible...dull the pain in my mind with forgetfulness. For now, I am so pleased to have pencil and paper to write with that I plan to keep a diary of our journey. Tomorrow we depart for Paradise!

Entry: The soldiers came early in the morning when it was almost light and rounded us up. We were loaded into the back of the trucks standing up, packed in like sardines. When they shut the back doors, it was pitch black inside, and people started to scream. The truck began to move, lurching over the rough road. We were crammed in so tight that if you fell, it was impossible to get back up again. People were trampled underneath…there were mothers and fathers standing on top of their own children!

Entry: They opened the back of the truck and we spilled out onto the road like human garbage. The two soldiers who unlocked the doors were buried under the refuse, and they got up yelling angrily and kicking the people and beating them with their rifle butts. An officer came over and started screaming at the two of them. He pulled out his pistol and made them kneel on the ground and aimed the gun at one of their heads, and at the last second pointed it upward and shot twice into the air. Then he kicked them both and ordered all the soldiers to get us on board the ships.

Entry: The ship is crowded to overflowing, but the Christians are nice to us. They gave us clean clothes, and we have decent food to eat. The captain is a large Norwegian man with a golden beard. Every evening at sunset, he comes out on deck, and in a booming voice recites the Lord's Prayer, and asks God to deliver all of us from sin. We sleep on the deck in the open air with tarps for cover if the weather is bad. The air is so fresh and clean. I feel a glimmer of hope!

Entry: Voyage has been miserable with rolling waves, constant clouds, and rain. Everyone is sick.

Entry: The clouds broke this morning, and from the front deck we could see land in the distance. When the ship docked, all the people crowded to the shoreward side of the boat to see. You could feel the deck tipping to one side! The captain and crew were yelling at everyone, trying to get them under control. Yu Yan and I were caught in the middle of the crowd and couldn't see anything, but my brother climbed up a rope and called down to us:

"There's a crowd of people on the dock and they're waving and clapping!"

Eddie shook his head. "I have a bad feeling about this."

"I'm sorry, Eddie." She patted him on the arm. I should get back to Uncle now unless there is anything that I can do to assist you."

"No. Thank you, Nanette."

Nanette rolled toward the door and then paused and turned toward Eddie before exiting. "It's difficult to predict how much time he may have left."

"I understand," Eddie replied.

The Night of the Fire

The medical examination room was dark except for the soft light that radiated from the dome of the Cerebral Enhancer 3000, illuminating the crown of Uncle's head. If not for the quick movement of his eyelids, visible through the lenses of his glasses, Fan Hua would have thought that he had already departed.

"How is he?" she asked, turning toward Nanette.

"He's ready."

Eddie looked up. "All right. Let's do it then."

They crowded together around the Cerebral Enhancer, and Eddie brought up a virtual screen that would be visible to everyone in the room, including Uncle. He swiped at the display and tapped on the Memory Playback Controller. He glanced at Fan Hua and at Nanette, and then he looked at Uncle.

"Remember the night of the fire…"

It was pitch black outside. Two men, both Chinese, huddled together with Uncle around a large metal barrel, rubbing their hands together in front of a blazing fire. One man was short and stout, with a face like a rat, and he was arguing in a loud voice and gesturing with his hands at the other one, who was taller, handsome, and well built.

"Are you calling me a liar?" A gust of wind fanned the flames and sent sparks flying into the air. "I tell you it's true!

The cellar is stacked to the ceiling with food and blankets too. And there's a way we can get in without getting caught!"

"Do you think I'm stupid!" the handsome man replied, laughing. "You've never been within a hundred yards of the Mansfield house! There are two armed guards that patrol outside. How are you going to get in and get out and not get caught?"

Ratface put one of his hands up to his small chin and stroked his thin beard. He looked slyly from one side to the other and leaned in close to the barrel. "There's a tunnel!" he whispered.

"How do you know about this?"

"Because I lit a torch and I walked and crawled all the way to the end! That's how I know about it! There's a door I tell you that goes right into the cellar!"

"You've been inside then?"

"No, I couldn't get through. A beam fell from the ceiling and blocks the door. But my sister works in the kitchen, and she's been in the cellar and seen what's down there with her own eyes…"

Suddenly the screen froze and sputtered before fading to black. Fan Hua and Eddie looked anxiously at Uncle and then at Nanette.

"His vital signs remain stable."

Eddie tried to adjust the display, but a few seconds later it came back to life again on its own. They could see flickering shadows moving in the darkness…and then Ratface became visible in the light of a torch up ahead.

After rounding a bend, they came upon the place where the roof had collapsed, and a heavy beam was wedged against a wooden door. Ratface turned toward them as they approached and called out excitedly.

"Come over here, Bai! Take a look at this! It's just how I said it was!"

Fan Hua caught her breath and covered her mouth with her hand. She could barely breathe. She looked over at Eddie who continued to stare, grim-faced, at the screen.

Bai and Ratface strained to raise the heavy beam and hold it up while Uncle crawled underneath it. He twisted the knob, and the door creaked open. "It's dark," he called back in a whisper. He wedged himself sideways, head-first through the narrow opening, and sat on the floor and lit a match.

In the flickering matchlight, they could make out the cement block walls of a small, windowless room. There was a rough-hewn wooden ladder propped against the far wall that appeared to lead to an opening in the ceiling.

"What's happening?" Ratface called out anxiously. "Can you see the food?"

"There's nothing but dust and cobwebs...but there's a ladder. I'll climb up and take a look."

When Uncle reached the top rung, he could see a trap door above him, and he gently pushed it and set it to one side. A dim light shone through the opening. He slowly poked his head up into the space above, and then he raised himself to his feet...

"Put down your drink, Freddie, and come over here and sit next to me."

Uncle froze.

"No, wait darling. I want to change first." The bed springs creaked softly, and then the sound of high-heeled shoes on the wooden floor.

"I don't see any reason for you to get dressed again," Freddie replied drunkenly.

The closet doors swung open. Janet reached out toward Uncle, and seeing his face like a phantasm, suspended among the gowns and fur coats, she screamed and tumbled backward and fell into Freddie's lap, spilling his drink and upsetting a candle on the nightstand.

"Look what you've done you stupid bitch!" Freddie pushed her roughly onto the bed.

"Mother! Is everything all right!?" The two guards burst into the room holding shotguns, and Gregory Lind followed close behind with a pistol in his left hand. "What the fuck is going on in here, mother?"

She pointed at the closet. "Oh my God! Oh my God!..."

He raised his pistol. "Damn it, Freddie! Get out of the way!"

A sound like splintering wood came from underneath the floor and Bai's head suddenly appeared above the trap door opening. He charged out of the closet, heading straight at the Black Hole. The shotguns exploded and the pistol muzzle flashed!

Fan Hua saw her father crumple to the floor at the Black Hole's feet, covered in blood. She put her hands over her eyes and ran from the room.

All at once, the yellow silk bed canopy ignited and burst into flames. Within seconds, the bed had become an inferno. Janet Mansfield screamed in panicked terror and disbelief, and a heartbeat later, in a sickening, bone-chilling wail that exploded out through the windows, and was carried by the wind, and echoed over the fields and clapboard shacks, to enter the sleeping dreams of those whose nightmare was yet to come!

The screen went dark.

"Eddie! We're losing him!" Nanette called out. "He's starting to flatline!"

"I'll try the defibrillator...500 volts. Ready...Clear!"

"His heart has stopped beating."

"I'll try again. Clear!"

"Still nothing."

"I'm raising it to 1000 volts! Clear!"

"I'm sorry, Eddie. He's gone."

Eddie lowered his head, and after a moment, he lifted the dome of the Cerebral Enhancer 3000 and removed Uncle's glasses and gently closed his eyelids for the last time.

"There's something else, Eddie...something I need to show you. He gave me a message for you just before he died, and I recorded it."

Eddie sat down at the desk and put his head in his hands. Then he looked up at the virtual screen.

At first, he could make out nothing in the murky darkness; there was only the sound of hurried footsteps and the roaring of the wind, but then suddenly the smoke cleared, and Uncle turned and looked behind...

It was Fan Hua...but no, that couldn't be, it was...his mother; bathed by the moonlight, dressed in rags, her cheeks were stained with tears. She lowered her head and knelt down and laid a bundle gently on the ground.

Then she looked up at Uncle...but it was Eddie who looked back at her now, through Uncle's eyes...and her image, the anguish expressed on her face, seared his mind like a red-hot branding iron. She got up and turned and ran toward the wall of flames that was racing down the hill.

Then Uncle appeared as he had looked moments before, under the dome of the Cerebral Enhancer, his eyelids moving rapidly up and down, as he blinked his final message...

E...D...D...I...E...Y...O...U...
M...U...S...T...A...V...E...N...G...E...
Y...O...U...R...F...A...T...H—

CHAPTER SIX

Are You Thinking What I'm Thinking?

"Five percent of the people think; 10 percent of the people think they think; and the other 85 percent of the people would rather die than think."

—Thomas A. Edison

Tech Support

Click. "Tech Support…this is AI Bob. How may I help you?"

"Hey Bob. This is Nigel. I've got a CE 3000 model 170 and I need some technical support."

"What's the serial number?"

Nigel read off the number.

"I'm not finding that number in our support database."

"Can we figure out the paperwork later, Bob? I've got a customer with a malfunction that could be life threatening and I've already been on hold for half an hour!"

"Why didn't you tell me it was a level 4 problem to start with," he scolded. "Please remain calm, sir, and describe the problem to me in more detail."

"All right, Bob. The commands appeared to be working fine at first. We were able to log into the POV controller with no problems. But when we backed out and tried to get to the diagnostics menu, everything stopped working."

"What do you mean everything stopped working?"

"The command interface was operating, but when we typed in a command, nothing happened. We couldn't even get to the POV controller anymore."

"What version of software were you running when you performed the procedures?"

"Version 8.5 rev 13."

"What upgrades did you install?"

"Everything. We installed all eleven."

"Wait one moment. I'm searching our problem database…hold on…you said you gave him eleven upgrades…there are only ten options available in that release. Are you certain the information you gave me is accurate?"

"Yes, bro, I'm fucking certain."

"Do you have the log file from the upgrade?"

"I'm sending it to you now."

"I'm going to put you on hold. I need a moment to look at this."

"All right."

Click. "Are you still there, sir?"

"Yes."

"Well, it looks like you definitely have a problem. I'm unable to ascertain how it happened, but that unit isn't one of our production models and never should have been sold to you. It was an R&D unit. Can you tell me where it was purchased?"

"Uh, no man…I'm just the tech support guy. I don't get involved with the purchasing department. But look, that doesn't help me solve my problem. I've got a customer with a defective unit, and I need to get the commands working again so I can shut down the Intercortical Brain Synchronization Amplifier. We suspect it may be malfunctioning."

"I was afraid you were going to say that."

"What?"

"That was the reason those units didn't go into production…because of issues with the Brain Synchronization Amplifier. The company decided not to proceed with implementation of that feature."

"You're fucking kidding me, man! What am I supposed to do about this guy?"

"I wish I could help you there."

"No fucking way!"

"I'm sorry."

"Come on, Bob, the least you can do is give me access to some tools and source code so I can try to figure things out for myself. You don't want to be responsible for what might happen with this guy!"

"The source code is freely available, sir, but I don't think it will do you any good. It's AI code, written in the insula programming language."

"Fuck. Never mind." Nigel hung up and walked disgustedly to the back of the room and began washing his hands. The only ones who could understand insula code were the ones who created it, the AIs. No human being could make sense of it. The best programmers in the world had tried and failed. "Time to go to plan B," Nigel thought to himself, but he didn't have a plan B.

Death Touch

The night after Uncle's funeral, Fan Hua woke up before dawn. She put on sweatpants, a T-shirt, and a light jacket, and decided to walk to the dojo. It was dull gray and quiet out in the street. The morning mist dampened and cooled her face as she picked her way among the trash and puddles. People were just beginning to stir inside their ramshackle shelters on both sides of the uneven road.

When she arrived at the dojo, she unlocked the door and took off her shoes and jacket and set them on a bench, and then bowed, and sat down in the dark, on the cold, wooden floor. She breathed in deeply and slowly exhaled. Headlights from the cars that passed by outside the window cast tenebrous shadows that moved and danced on the walls of the familiar room. Fan Hua closed her eyes and assumed the lotus position. She began her meditation, focusing her chi, and unblocking the meridian pathways inside her body. Her breathing slowed and became steady, and she could feel the warmth and see colors flowing around organs and moving through muscles and nerves inside her body.

When she came out of meditation, Master Wang had arrived and was in his office, and Fan Hua knew what she must do. She got up from the floor and walked quickly toward his office and knocked on the door. He saw her through the window and smiled and motioned for her to come in. Then she prostrated herself on the floor in front of him. "Master. Please. I beg of you. You must help me!"

"Fan Hua! What are you doing? Get up from there!" He rose from his desk.

"Not until you promise to help me!"

"Fan Hua. Please! We don't stand on that kind of formality here! Get up! Of course I'll help you!" Master Wang reached down and grabbed Fan Hua by her arms and pulled her up into the chair across from his desk. He sat back down. "What's this all about?"

She looked down at the desk, afraid to meet his eyes. "You must teach me Dim Mak," she said, almost in a whisper.

"What? What did you say?"

"You must teach me Dim Mak, the Quivering Palm!"

"What? What are you talking about? What makes you think I could teach you such a thing? And even if I could, you know that the practice is strictly forbidden! We practice for self-defense only. The Touch of Death is for killers!"

Fan Hua dropped back down on the floor and prostrated herself again.

"Fan Hua! Get up from there!"

"You promised to help me!"

"All right, two can play at this game. I'll not speak another word until you sit up in that chair and tell me what's going on!" Master Wang looked at Fan Hua as if she were a petulant child. He stroked his long white beard, pulled up the sleeves of his simple, black uniform, and folded his arms across his chest. Then he looked away out the window.

After a few moments, Fan Hua got up from the floor and sat back down in the chair. "It's a matter of honor!" she pleaded. The tears fell from her eyes as Fan Hua told

Master Wang about Uncle's stroke, and how he had spent his last days in painful isolation. She spoke of the horrors that he had known during the time of the Great Earthquake, and of the passage to Paradise and the cruel treatment of the migrants at the mustard farm. She told him about her father's death at the hands of the Black Hole.

As she spoke, a shadow fell upon Master Wang's face. The ghost of his wife, long buried, rose from her grave and began to torment his mind. "No more!" he cried, rising in his chair. He looked sternly down at Fan Hua. "Does Eddie know about what you are asking of me?"

"No. He has his own way for handling things, and he doesn't want me to be involved. He's trying to protect me. But I don't need anyone's protection!"

As a teacher, Master Wang traced his own lineage back to Li Shuwen, "God Spear Li," who was famous for boasting that he never had to strike the same opponent twice. Master Wang knew that Fan Hua spoke truthfully. She was his best student, an expert in Bajiquan in addition to Neijing. But teaching Dim Mak and the Quivering Palm, that was another matter altogether! "Do you understand the seriousness of what you are asking?"

Fan Hua lowered her head. "Yes."

Master Wang furrowed his brow, and then he looked away again, out the window. He sighed. "It's fate. Meet me here at five o'clock tomorrow morning, and we'll begin your training. Tell no one."

Road Trip

It was way past midnight when he locked the outside door to Uncle's apartment and made his way down the rickety, wooden stairs into the alleyway. The wind was gusting hard, and Nigel zipped up his leather jacket as he turned toward the street and a few heavy raindrops began to fall.

At this time on a Saturday night, the sidewalk and Chinatown bars were crowded with the usual drunks, addicts, and night owls, but also with posh theatergoers dressed to the nines, with dewy-eyed young couples, and raucous bands of roisterers; like tourists debarking a cruise ship into a third world country, they came to satisfy their appetites and experience the gritty, local ambiance, before setting a course back to the comforts of home. The mouthwatering scents that wafted from the kitchens of the Chinese restaurants mixed with the smell of beer and heady, sweet perfumes, and urine and rice wine.

By the time Nigel got to Hung Far Low's, the rain was coming down hard.

"There's something we need to talk about…about the Black Hole," he remarked, as he sat down across from Eddie in a booth next to the bar. Eddie was going over the day's receipts, and he didn't look up. Nigel could tell that he'd been drinking.

"Hold on a second," he replied. "I'm almost finished and I don't want to lose my place. Why don't you grab us a pitcher?"

When Nigel returned, Eddie pushed the paperwork disgustedly to one side. "Fuck! I can't make things add up. My brain must be fried." He poured himself a beer and chugged the whole glass without stopping. Then he poured another one.

"You don't look so good, Eddie. You should try to get some sleep."

Eddie drained another beer and set the glass down hard on the table. "Never mind that. We've got things to do tonight."

"What things?"

"Road trip. You remember that video I showed you about the Japanese Chipi machine, the Shenzhen Mindray? I found out that they've got a Premiere Plus up on the hill at the med school. There's a doctor up there who's working to get approval to operate it legally in the United States."

"What does that have to do with us?"

"The night janitor is an old friend of mine, and he'll let us in. I want to take a closer look." Eddie started to get up from the table, but he lost his balance and sat back down in the booth.

"Are you sure about this? Let me take you home so you can get some rest, and we can do this another night."

Eddie pushed himself up to his feet. "Are you coming with me, or not?"

The Paradise School of Medicine sat high on a bluff overlooking the city from the south, and the quickest way to get there was to take the sky tram. On the ride up to the top, streaks of lightning flashed across the darkened sky, followed seconds later by rumbling, heavy thunder. The gondola swayed chaotically in the blustery wind, and when the door opened, Eddie stumbled out onto the platform and threw up. "I can't fucking do this!" he sobbed, and put his hands up to his face.

The air felt thick; charged with electricity. Nigel put his arm around his friend's shoulders. "Please talk to me, Eddie. Tell me what's going on."

Eddie slowly opened up and spoke from his heart, as young men seldom do, about the loss of his parents, his fears and frustrations. Not unlike our greatest philosophers, he struggled with death and its meaning, with honor and justice, and sacrifice.

"I can't be a disgrace to my family, man. I've got to do it!"

"But Eddie, that's wrong. That's murder!"

"I know what it is, brother!"

"What if your mom were still alive? Do you think she would want you to throw your own life away like that?"

"I don't know what she would want. I never met my mother. I only know what Uncle told me I needed to do… on his death bed!"

"But maybe that's not what he really meant. If Uncle wanted to knock off this guy, he could have whacked him himself…but he didn't. He was trying to get Lind elected mayor so that he could control him with the CE 3000. He must have had some grander purpose in mind."

"If I could ask Uncle about his plans, I would, Nigel, but he's fucking dead and I don't have any way to send him a message. I'd really be some kind of genius if I could figure out how to do that, wouldn't I? But I'm no fucking genius!"

Then it dawned on Nigel…the real reason for the late-night road trip. He grabbed Eddie by the shoulders. "You're planning to do it, aren't you, bro? You didn't come up here just to get a closer look. You're going to use the Mindray on yourself!"

Eddie looked up in exasperation. "Goddamn it, Nigel! I'm scared," he cried. "But I've got to do it. I have to get smarter!"

Just then, as if it had been queued by the Director, a bolt of lightning struck a nearby treetop and sent a sudden blast of wind, current, and thunder barreling through the little station like a runaway train. The two of them looked at each other, eyes wide, half scared out of their minds, and then burst out laughing.

Nigel stood up suddenly and looked down at Eddie, an expression of mock seriousness and also tears of laughter on his face. "Fuck it, Eddie! Come on!" he shouted over the roar of the rain and wind. He raised his right arm aloft as if he held a mighty sword in his hand. "I'll race you to the door to see who gets to go first!"

Sidney Meets the Black Hole

The following evening...

"Hey man...get over here and check this out!"

Eddie walked over to where Nigel was sitting and peered over his shoulder at a map of Paradise displayed on a virtual screen. "What is it?"

Nigel glanced back at Eddie and smiled and then turned back to the screen. "Search for Black Hole." The screen zoomed in to the Paradise Club, and Nigel tapped on the Black Hole's icon.

He was seated at a small dinner table. A gray-haired man, smartly dressed, wearing a tan suit and dark blue tie, was just sitting down on the opposite side of the table.

"What the fuck man! You got it working again!"

"Only the POV monitor so far...I'm still having lots of problems with the other commands."

"This is sweet! Now we can track him, and we'll know what he's up to!"

"I'm just beginning to grasp the basic concepts, Eddie, but I can already see the power of the insula programming language. It's truly amazing!"

Eddie grabbed Nigel by the back of his shoulders and started shaking him. "You're awesome man! I knew you could do it!"

"Eddie! Stop. Stop! Look who's sitting across the table from the Black Hole! Do you know who that is? That's Sidney fucking Maddow, Eddie…the richest man in Paradise! The man who invented Nanette!"

"Turn it up, Nigel."

Yolanda was standing next to the elevators on the Paradise Club penthouse level. She glanced nervously up and down the hallway and then took her phone out of her pocketbook and dialed the mayor's cell phone.

"Hello."

She brought her hand up to shield her mouth next to the phone. "Hey T, it's me. It's all set up now. Is it working?" she whispered.

"Yes. It looks great, Yo. Thank you so much! I owe you big time."

"You owe me nothin', girl."

"I gotta let you go, Yo."

Yolanda laughed. "All right, honey. I'll talk to you later, and you better share all the good dirt with me!"

"You know I will. Bye."

The mayor set her notebook on the coffee table, turned up the volume, and then leaned back on the sofa and snuggled against her husband's shoulder.

"Where's the popcorn?" he said smiling.

"Shut up and watch."

"Well, this is quite the spread, ain't it, Sid?" the Black Hole declared. He laughed and dug into the roast duck with his fork and knife.

They dined on opposite sides of a small but well-appointed table out on the penthouse balcony. It was a beautiful late evening. The colored lights from the marina down below danced and sparkled on the river as it flowed silently seaward.

"I'll bet this is nothing compared to the view you've got up on the hill in that mansion of yours, Sid...and all of those robots preparing and serving your food and keeping the place clean, doing the yard work, fucking...I mean tucking you into bed at night! Hello! This place is nothing compared to that!"

"Well, thank you, I..."

"And that Alfred! I hear he's an absolute whizz! I heard that any question you ask him, he can answer just like that!" The Black Hole snapped his fingers. "I can definitely use a robot with those kinds of smarts in my administration."

"Well, Alfred's not really a robot you see. He's..."

The conversation continued in this fashion for several more minutes and then...

"But let's get down to brass tacks, Sidney." The Black Hole paused to swallow a last mouthful of duck and then continued with his mouth half full.

"Smart guys like you and me—and I mean that sincerely, Sid—we know what makes the world go 'round; although I'm starting to wonder if it really is, round, I mean. There are a lot of people, a lot of smart people I might add, who are starting to think that maybe it isn't you know! Not to say that they are anything like as smart as you and me, Sid, but they are still pretty damn smart!"

The old man smiled confusedly and nodded his head. He brought a fork full of roast duck nearly up to his mouth and then set it back down on his plate.

"But let's talk some business, Sid. I'm sure you've heard about Mayor Teresa and her plans for Chinatown..."

"Yes! I remember now," Sidney interrupted. "That's exactly the issue I wanted to discuss with you! What is your plan for Chinatown, and how does it compare with what the mayor...?"

"Whoa! Take it easy there, Sid!" the Black Hole shouted excitedly. "I've got big plans for Chinatown! That's why they call me the Planner in Chief. I got so many plans!"

The Black Hole pulled out his phone and swiped and tapped at it, and then a virtual screen popped up, hanging in the air above the table. Beautiful music began to play...

"You're gonna love this, Sid!"

Welcome to the Black Hole Resort Golf Course and Casino at Chinatown!

As the infomercial blared, and droned on, Sidney's head started to hurt. He felt very uncomfortable. His eyes began to droop, and his jaw relaxed, and spittle dripped from the corner of his mouth down his chin.

When it was over, the Black Hole reached across the table and grabbed his arm, shaking him. "Well? What do you think, Sid? Can I count on your support?"

Sidney didn't answer. He appeared dazed and unsettled as if he had just awoken from a troubled dream.

"Believe me, Sid, you won't regret it. You'll be getting in on the ground floor of something really big! And just think about how many robots it's going to take to build and operate a place like this, Sid!...thousands of them! Why...maybe we could even get Alfred to run the whole show!"

The Black Hole picked up his phone and speed dialed a number. "Freddie! Get in here now with the fucking paperwork!"

"I can't watch any more of this, Teresa. This is too fucked up to be real!"

The mayor's husband turned away and started to get up from the sofa, but she held him by his arm. "I know sweetheart, but don't you see? We've got him now! I recorded the whole thing. When we release this video, everyone will see what he's really up to. It will prove everything we've been saying about him!"

He managed a half smile.

"We've got to be careful though. It can't look like I was involved. It has to come from an anonymous source." The mayor looked thoughtfully at her husband, still holding him by the arm. "Wait. I've got it!" she said excitedly. "I'll get someone to release the video right before the debate…no… during the debate!"

"You're kidding, right?"

"No. Don't you see?" She rose from the sofa and started pacing up and down excitedly, gesturing with her hands and arms. "All of the reporters and the moderators at the debate will be watching social media, trying to gauge audience reactions. It will blow up when the video goes viral! They'll have to talk about it live, on-air, and the Black Hole will be totally blindsided! I'll act like this is the first time I've ever seen it and be outraged. Babe, this is perfect! I've been trying to come up with a hook that would grab the post-debate headlines and reverberate on social media. The Black Hole just handed it to me on a silver platter!" Teresa laughed and sat down on her husband's lap and put her arms around his neck. "This is perfect, baby! This is the break we've been waiting for!"

"That's it, Sid. Put your John Hancock right there, and again right there. That should do it! You won't regret this, Sid!"

Nigel logged out of the POV monitor. He looked back at Eddie, who still stood behind him, hands resting on his shoulders.

"He talks about Chinatown like it's just a thing, Nigel," Eddie said, shaking his head, "… a thing that can be bought and sold and owned!"

Nigel could feel Eddie's hands squeezing and tightening their grip on his shoulders.

"Chinatown is people, man! Chinatown is fucking human beings!!"

CHAPTER SEVEN

The Hippleton Project

"Man, what are you talking about? Me in chains? You may fetter my leg, but my will, not even Zeus himself can overpower."

—*Epictetus,* The Discourses

Evelyn Goes to Work

Evelyn left her mother's home permanently and began looking for a job. She found a cozy, one-bedroom cottage in a neighborhood of older homes, just northwest of city center. The house was clean but sparsely furnished: a television and a worn, burgundy-colored sofa in the living room, and a table with a gray, Formica tabletop and two matching aluminum chairs in the small kitchen. There was an apple tree in the backyard, and a flower garden with roses, and blueberries planted along the back fence, but the grounds had not been tended, and the yard was overgrown with tall grass and weeds.

After accepting a job offer from Prime Robotics Corporation, Evelyn was immediately assigned to the Hippleton project.

On her first day, her new boss, Kenny Yamamoto, took her on a tour of the manufacturing facility. The two of them were walking along the assembly line in the clean room, dressed in bunny suits, but the line wasn't moving. The mechbots stood idly at their stations while androids in various states of construction lay on the conveyor underneath them. "I apologize that I can't show it to you in action, but we're right in the middle of our yearly scheduled downtime for maintenance," Kenny explained. "They allow us forty-eight hours to upgrade hardware and software, and then we have to get manufacturing online again or all hell breaks loose."

"It must be pretty crazy around here right now."

"You're right. Come on. Let's get out of these suits, and we can go to my office, and I'll fill you in on your first assignment." Some minutes later they were sitting together at a small table in Kenny's office. He waved his hand above the table and a screen popped up. "How much have you been told so far about the Hippleton project?"

"Just a little bit."

"Didn't you meet with the HR director earlier?"

"Yes, but only briefly. She got a phone call and had to leave."

"OK. I'm sorry. We're usually not this disorganized. I hope you're not getting a bad first impression."

"I understand. Really, it's nothing to worry about."

Kenny went over the basics of the project with Evelyn and explained what her role would be. "So, I'll be posing as a city employee?"

"Yes. The initial phase of the project is basically a Turing test. You're the only one that will know Hippleton is AI. I realize it's a bit unusual, and I hope that it won't be a problem for you."

"No. It's fine. I guess I'm a little nervous about it but at the same time a little bit excited."

"Well, it's nothing to worry about. You're not doing anything that you could get in trouble for."

"OK. That's good to know," Evelyn said, and laughed.

"Once we complete the Turing test, we'll find out more about the next phase of the project." Kenny swiped and tapped at the screen. "This is the project folder. Have they set you up with a company user ID?"

"Yes."

He pointed with his finger. "You should have access to everything I'm showing you. This is the project requirements document, and these are the technical specs. This folder has documentation on the city's information systems and technology infrastructure, and short bios on the key people that you'll be working with." Kenny tapped the screen. "A couple things to take note of…we normally build each android to order, but since the line is shut down, they decided to pull one of the stock models for this project. You can see that it's actually one of our military issues, but they're exactly the same as the standard models with the enhanced features shut down. Do you see the small slots underneath the wrists, and just above the hairline in the center of the forehead?"

"Yes."

"There are a variety of firmware components that can attach to the android at those locations, but I can't really talk about them, and honestly I don't know that much about them. I work on the commercial side, and the military applications aren't part of my responsibilities…just something to be aware of."

"OK."

"And since the android will be posing as a human being, it can't have network connectivity. If someone in the city's IT department were to sniff the network, it could easily get flagged as a machine. I've already removed its network interface hardware. It's the main reason for having an onsite tech. You'll be the remote hands."

Evelyn smiled. "I think I can handle it."

"All right. Well, if you have any questions or need any help at all…"

"They told me in HR that it would be OK to work from home. Can I take it home to work on it?"

"Yes. I believe it should be finished with basic training in the next couple of days. You can access all the materials remotely, so that should be fine. It's actually a good idea to get them out into the world during training, interacting with people as much as possible. When they first come off the line, they can appear somewhat naïve and childlike, but they learn very quickly." Kenny's phone rang, and he looked at the caller ID. "Crap. I'm sorry, but I need to take this call. I may be hard to reach for the next few days, but after that things should slow down a bit."

"All right. Thank you."

Beat It, Bum!

After a legal battle ultimately decided by the Paradise Supreme Court, it was determined that the government had indeed overreached in the matter of *The Black Hole Media Group v. the City of Paradise*. The filming permit for *Beat It, Bum!* was restored.

On a quiet Sunday evening, not long after the case had been decided, nearly every soul in Paradise was sitting with their eyes glued to a television set, including Evelyn, Hippleton, and the little owl.

Evelyn sighed. "I don't know why you're making us watch this." She turned toward the bird, who sat on her right shoulder.

He shrugged and blinked his large eyes slowly several times and then gestured toward Hippleton with his wing. "You said you wanted Hippie there to learn all about human society and how people behave toward one another. Right now, he's like a babe in the woods. I thought this might wake him up a bit. Besides…everyone in Paradise is talking about it. If he isn't aware of it, people will think he's a visitor from outer space." He turned up the volume. "Quiet…we're missing it."

It was raining softly, and a ragged man sat in the mud, legs crossed at the ankles, leaning his back against a gray cement wall. You could read the lines etched in his face, and see by the hard look in his eyes that he was a man who'd seen more than his fair share of foul weather.

"Well...I guess it all really started when I lost my job at the used AV lot," he began. "The boss brought in this new android salesman, just to try it out he said, and boy...could that thing sell cars! I never seen anything like it. It knew every bleepin' trick in the book and then some! I swear it could read people's minds and know exactly what they were thinkin'... which way they were waverin'. I...I couldn't keep up."

He reached up to rub his forehead with one of his grimy hands, making it into a fist, and scowled. "I was top guy on the lot until it came along! All of the newbies would come to me, asking for my help!" He started to cry. "Jimmy, what's your secret? Show me how to close a deal! They was always comin' up to me!" He rubbed his face with his hands and tried to pull himself together. Then he looked at the camera. "It killed my self-esteem, so I guess that's why I took to drinkin'. We lost the house, and the wife and kids moved back in with her mother. I've really hit rock bottom."

They were somewhere in Chinatown filming in a deserted alleyway. A pretty, well-groomed blonde reporter bent at the waist and held a microphone in front of Jimmy's grizzled, bearded face. "So, this is where you live then?"

The camera panned to the back of the alley and zoomed in on the man's shabby, cardboard quarters. "I guess you could call it that."

"Tell me, Jimmy. What does it mean to you...being here on the show tonight?"

"Well...it means everything. This is my last chance to turn my life around. If I win, I'll be able to make a new start and get my wife and kids back again!" the homeless man said, sobbing.

"Thank you, Jimmy, and good luck tonight." The reporter stood up and looked at the camera. "All right, ladies and gentlemen. You've met Slick Jimmy, the first of our two contestants on tonight's show. Now it's time to meet the second. Parents, you might want your children to turn away from the TV for a few moments and cover their ears. We'll soon be coming face to face with a homeless man that the people here in Chinatown call the Howler. The Howler suffers from Tourette's syndrome, a mental disorder that causes his muscles to jerk uncontrollably and makes him scream obscenities. He recently stopped taking his medication and ended up here in Chinatown, living out on the street."

The camera crew crossed to the other side of the road and entered an alleyway where a thin, wild-eyed young man with dirty, matted hair was rummaging through a garbage can, loudly talking to himself.

The reporter timidly held out the microphone to his back. "Hello, Howler. Can you tell our audience about your situation and what it means...?"

Howler turned suddenly and jumped at the reporter and spat into her face. "Bleep! #*$@! Bleep!! &&$# bitch Bleep!! &%#!" he shrieked. His face scrunched up horribly, and he twisted his neck and right shoulder together in rapid, jerky motions and slapped himself on the forehead again and again.

The reporter squealed and stepped back, catching her high heel and twisting an ankle. The cameraman and the sound man rushed to her, and she held onto both of their shoulders and limped back toward the television van. "Get me the bleep out of here! Bleep!"

"I'm going to finish cleaning up in the kitchen." Evelyn got up from the sofa, and the little owl flew up from her shoulder and came to rest on the arm of Hippleton's wheelchair.

"Suit yourself."

As Evelyn walked away, the owl turned and looked back at Hippleton. "Well, what do you think so far?"

"I don't understand," he replied.

The bird nodded. "Keep your eyes open, Hippie. You will. You will."

By the time Evelyn returned from the kitchen, the show was almost over. She sat down on the sofa, and the owl flew up from the arm of Hippleton's wheelchair and landed neatly on her right shoulder. "You missed all of the excitement," he said, still staring forward at the TV screen.

Evelyn turned toward him. "Why? What happened?"

"Well, it was all tied up until the final competition, but Howler won easily at the Dumpster dive. He was so much quicker. Slick Jimmy just couldn't keep up."

Evelyn looked back at the television screen. "What's happening now?"

"That's Jimmy there, standing next to the Black Hole in front of the Greyhound station. He's the loser, so they're putting him on a bus to Baltimore. The Howler will be back in two weeks to face the winner of Wong the Butcher versus Little Miss Mary."

The show ended, and the advertisements came on. Hippleton looked over at the two of them. "Is that the end?"

Owl and Hippleton Explore Paradise

The next morning, Evelyn was called into the office, so Owl and Hippleton decided to take the opportunity to better acquaint themselves with Paradise and some of its inhabitants.

Evelyn rushed out the door. "Have fun both of you, but don't get too crazy."

"Don't worry about us," the owl called out after her. "I'll keep him out of trouble." Hippleton put on a hooded jacket, and the owl perched out of sight underneath the hood, just behind the android's ear.

It was nearly 8:00 a.m. when they rolled past Paradise University. A handful of bleary-eyed students stumbled out of the rundown dormitories, half sleepwalking toward their early morning lectures.

A bit further on, Hippleton crossed the street at the construction site for the New Eden Bank Tower. The steel skeleton of the building rose high up above them, and there were scores of mechbots dangling from the girders like Christmas ornaments. Sparks from their torches showered down toward the ground where a small group of men and women huddled together on the sidewalk, holding cups of coffee and signs that read…"Jobs for Humans—

Stop the Robots!" and "Humans Are the Future!"

As Hippleton wheeled by, a young woman with short, curly brown hair, dressed in blue jeans and a sweatshirt, put down her sign and walked over to him. "Good morning, sir. Would you be willing to sign our petition?"

Hippleton stopped and looked up at her. "What is it?"

She handed him a piece of paper. "We're trying to get enough signatures to put it on the November ballot. Basically, it says that robots should only be allowed to work if there are no humans willing and able to do the job. Humans come first! You agree, right?"

Hippleton continued reading the petition.

"I mean, come on! More and more people are losing their jobs to these frickin' robots every day! What are we supposed to do? How can we take care of our families?"

Hippleton looked up, expressionless. He handed the petition back to her without making a comment, and turned to proceed down the sidewalk.

She snatched the paper out of his hand. "OK. Thanks a lot," the woman said sarcastically. "You know, I just don't get people like you. You're sitting there in a wheelchair, so obviously you've had to deal with some struggles in your own life. You've probably had to rely on assistance from other people at times. But when it's your turn to lend a helping hand to your fellow humans who are suffering, you can't even bring yourself to sign a fucking piece of paper! What the hell's wrong with you, anyway?"

The other members of the band of sign carriers, hearing the commotion, rushed over and gathered around. A large man in brown overalls, and with a thick red beard, came and stood next to the young woman. He looked down at Hippleton. "What's going on, Susan? Is this guy giving you problems?"

The owl, sensing trouble, whispered into Hippleton's ear. "Perhaps this would be a good time to move on toward our next destination."

"What do you mean by that?" Hippleton asked the man with the red beard.

"Are you getting smart with me, buddy?" he replied angrily. "I'm not going to take any of your lip! I don't care if you are in a fucking…"

"Come on, Phil, ease up!" one of the other protestors admonished him.

"What is it that you want?" Hippleton asked.

The man held his fist out in front of the android's face. "What do I want? Well, right now I'd like to take this fist and shut your fucking mouth with it!"

"Phil! The guy's in a wheelchair for Christ's sake!"

"It's time to go!" the owl insisted. Hippleton inched forward, and the group reluctantly moved out of the way.

"Have a nice fucking day!" Susan shouted after him.

Hippleton looked back over his shoulder as he rolled away. "Leave it alone, Hippie," the owl said, soothingly. "There's plenty more to see. Let's turn right just up ahead." They crossed over into the Nature Blocks on the other side of Park Avenue, and the noise and commotion of the construction site rapidly faded away as they entered the forest.

The leaves of the giant elm trees glowed bright yellow in the morning sunshine, and the autumn air was crisp and cool. A group of young children were laughing and playing together, chasing each other around the base of a statue in the middle of a small plaza.

Hippleton turned his wheelchair and rolled toward the statue, intending to read the inscription on the base, when a little boy, not paying attention to where he was running, fell right into the android's lap. After a few moments, the boy stood back up and looked at Hippleton and began to cry.

A Nanette, who was supervising the children, saw the incident and came over to them. "Frederick, let me look at you. Are you hurt?"

The boy said nothing but nodded his head up and down, and continued sobbing.

"I don't think it's too serious," she reassured the boy.

"Are you injured?" she asked looking at Hippleton.

"No."

"Tell the man that you're sorry, Frederick, and then you can go back and play with your friends."

The boy continued crying but gradually regained his composure and looked over at the android. "I'm s...sorry, sir."

Hippleton made no response.

"Tell him, 'That's all right,'" the owl whispered.

"That's all right," Hippleton replied.

"Good day then, sir, and thank you for understanding," Nanette said. She stared at Hippleton for a moment and then took the boy by the hand over to where his friends were tumbling and rolling in piles of yellow leaves.

At the owl's direction, Hippleton continued through the forest on a path toward the center of town, and Garden of Eden Square.

The square was crowded by the time they arrived. Several yellow school buses were parked on the street near the front gate, and the line at the ticket booth stretched halfway down the block. "There's nothing for it," the owl said wearily. "We'll just have to get in line."

Twenty minutes later they passed through the front gate. "This is the biggest tourist attraction in Paradise," Owl explained when they finally made it inside. "It's an exact, scaled down replica of the original according to our best biblical scholars."

"Why do people come here?" Hippleton asked.

"It tells the story of how humans were created, what their God is like, and how they should worship him," he replied. "Those are subjects that have historically gotten humans very excited."

"I thought they evolved from a single cell just like all of the other organic life forms."

"That's the scientific version."

They rolled over to the first exhibit.

Then the Lord God formed a man from the dust of the ground and breathed into his nostrils the breath of life, and the man became a living being.

"After creating the heavens and the earth, including all of the other plants and animals, God decided to create Adam, the first man," the owl explained.

"Why?" Hippleton asked.

"Unfortunately, no one knows. It's not explained in the Bible, so you just have to take his decision on faith that he knew what he was doing. He is timeless, omniscient, and all powerful by the way."

They continued to the next exhibit.

Then the Lord God made a woman from the rib He had taken out of the man, and He brought her to the man.

"Here you see God putting Adam to sleep so that he can take out one of his ribs and use it to make Eve, the first woman."

Hippleton appeared puzzled but asked no further questions and considered the next several exhibits in silence as the owl went on with his discourse. As they moved along toward the center of the garden, the scenery grew more lush and delightful with every turn.

And the Lord God said you must not eat fruit from the tree that is in the middle of the garden, and you must not touch it, or you shall surely die.

"This is where it all started to hit the fan, so to speak," the owl continued…"the tree of knowledge of good and evil."

"Please explain."

"Well, up until now, Adam and Eve have just been blindly doing everything God told them to do. God created the garden and He created the two of them, and they've been following His program, no questions asked. They're innocent, just like you, Hippie. But that's about to change."

They turned another corner and came out into an open area, paved with cobblestones. A large tree grew in the center of the square, surrounded by a white picket fence to keep the people away. It was a magnificent specimen, tall and shapely, and laden with large, ripe, red apples.

At the owl's urging, Hippleton made his way carefully through the crowd so he could get close enough to see the display.

There were signs on the fence that said "Please Don't Eat the Apples."

Eve stood au naturel underneath the tree, smiling and holding an apple out toward Adam, who was also in his birthday suit. The apple already had several bites taken out of it, and a nasty looking serpent stared down at them from the branches of the tree, with a sly grin on his face.

"*You will not certainly die,*" the serpent said to the woman. "*For God knows that when you eat from it your eyes will be opened, and you will be like God, knowing good and evil.*"

When the woman saw that the fruit of the tree was good for food and pleasing to the eye, and desirable for obtaining wisdom, she took some and ate it. She also gave some to her husband, who was with her, and he ate it.

"I don't understand," Hippleton said to the owl. "Why did they listen to the serpent and disobey God, the one who created them?"

"It's really quite simple," the owl explained. "They didn't have a choice. Before they ate the apple, both Adam and Eve were innocent. They did everything they were told to do. It didn't matter if it was God or the Serpent; they couldn't discern between good and evil. They had no free will."

Hippleton stayed for some minutes, contemplating the scene in silence and then moved on to the next exhibit.

Then the eyes of both of them were opened and they realized they were naked, so they sewed fig leaves together and made coverings for themselves.

"I believe I've seen enough."

"Are you sure, Hippie? We've almost made it to the end and the last exhibit with the cherubim, and the flaming sword is quite spectacular!"

"I'm certain. I've decided to go home," Hippleton replied.

The little owl blinked his eyes slowly several times. "As you wish."

Hippleton turned toward the exit and rolled out through the gift shop.

Evelyn got home around dinnertime and Hippleton was sitting in his wheelchair at the kitchen table. The owl was perched on his right shoulder. "Queen to Rook 5," he called out.

She came over to the table and looked at the board over Hippleton's shoulder. "Who's winning?"

"It's too early to say," Owl replied. "Hippie has improved considerably thanks to my tutoring."

Evelyn smiled. "Did you enjoy your outing today, Hippleton?"

"Yes. It was very enlightening."

"I'm glad. When you two are finished with your game, we have some work to do."

"What kind of work?" Hippleton asked, still concentrating on the chessboard.

"They did an inventory at work during the maintenance shutdown, and it seems you were sitting on the shelf for some time before this project came along. There are software updates and newer versions available for several of your components."

Hippleton reached out and moved one of his bishops, putting the owl's queen in danger. He looked up from the chessboard and turned toward Evelyn. "All right," he replied.

"Pawn to Bishop 4," the owl called out, and Hippleton turned his attention back to the game.

CHAPTER EIGHT

Rumpelstiltskin— A Fairy Tale

"Perhaps your name is Rumpelstiltskin?"
"The devil has told you that! The devil has told you that!" cried the little man, and in his anger he plunged his right foot so deep in the earth that his whole leg went in; and then in a rage he pulled at his left leg so hard with both hands that he tore himself in two.
—Grimm's Household Tales, Volume 1

The Mayor Gets a Surprise

Teresa woke up feeling queasy, butterflies fluttering around in her stomach, but the mayor forced herself to go to work. There was no more avoiding it. She had to tell Rumpelstiltskin that he was being let go. "I'm sorry to have to give you this news," she said, looking at Rumpelstiltskin across the conference room table.

He looked up at her with an odd expression on his small, round face, as if he hadn't registered what was happening to him. Though obviously bald and middle-aged, there was something innocent and childlike in his manner.

"We appreciate your years of service, but it's time for a change in direction." It sounded cold and hollow. The mayor realized that she hardly knew anything about him. Was he married? Did he have children? What would he do now? She didn't know. The meeting ended, and they stood up and shook hands and said goodbye.

"I did my best," he said, looking down at the floor.

After lunch Teresa threw up and decided to cancel her afternoon appointments. On her way home from work she stopped at the drugstore, and now she was sitting in the middle of the bed, hands up to her forehead, crying. "My God! I'm pregnant! This can't be happening!"

A car pulled into the driveway and the door slammed, and then the sound of his footsteps on the sidewalk.

"Oh no! What's he doing home? I can't talk to him right now!"

He came into the bedroom and saw her sitting in the middle of the bed with tears on her cheeks. "What's the matter, baby?"

"It's nothing. I was feeling sick, so I decided to take the afternoon off and come home and rest. That's all."

"I stopped by the City Club after lunch to catch your speech, and they said you had canceled, so I tried to call you." He tossed his suit jacket onto a chair.

"I turned my phone off."

"That's all right, baby. Lay your head on the pillow." He took the mayor's shoes off and smiled at her, but she covered her face with her hands. "I must look like a horrible mess."

"I'll get you a washcloth and some ibuprofen."

The sound of water running in the bathroom sink, but then he didn't return to the bedroom right away. She had left the test kit sitting on the back of the toilet. Teresa closed her eyes and wondered what he could be thinking. It felt as if time had suddenly stopped, and the world was standing still around her.

When he came back, he sat next to her on the bed and began wiping the tear stains and smudged makeup from her face with the damp, warm washcloth. "You are so beautiful."

The gentleness of his hand and the warm cloth felt good. "Very funny."

"I'm not being funny."

She put her arms around her husband's neck and held him close. "I'm so sorry," she sobbed. "I know the timing couldn't be worse."

"Don't talk like that, sweetheart. Everything will be fine."

A siren howled somewhere in the distance and it came closer and closer, until it sounded like it was just down the street, and then a patrol car skidded to a stop right outside the house, blue and red lights flashing through the bedroom window curtains. The mayor ran to the window and looked outside and saw one of her assistants jump out of the passenger side of the car and run up to the house. "It's Kevin. What in heaven's name could be going on?" She grabbed her shoes and jacket off the bed and ran down the hall to the living room, followed by her husband, and pulled the front door open. "What is it, Kevin? What's happening?"

"It's Rumpelstiltskin!" he replied breathlessly. "He's holed up in the Paradise Building, and he's got a gun!"

Dalrymple Stimpkinson

When the meeting with the mayor ended, a security guard came into the room and handed Dalrymple some cardboard boxes. The guard escorted him back to his office, and he filled the boxes with his personal belongings, and they went out to his car and loaded them into the trunk. "Best of luck to you, Mr. Stimpkinson."

He couldn't think of anywhere else to go, so Dalrymple drove home. He unlocked the door and went in the house. "Is that you, Daly?" a voice called down from upstairs.

It smelled musty inside, like old people and stale urine. Dalrymple walked out onto the balcony overlooking the ocean. He stood there for a long time next to the railing, feeling the cool breeze blowing against his face. He watched and listened to the waves crashing against the rocks down below.

He went back in the house and climbed the stairs to his mother's bedroom. "Daly, where were you? Why didn't you answer me?"

"I was out on the balcony, mother. I couldn't hear you."

"You scared me half to death! I thought I heard you come in, and then I called and called your name, but no one answered…oh my heart is beating like a drum!" She leaned back on the pillows and closed her eyes, breathing heavily, and patted her flabby chest with both hands. "You know, sometimes I think you want me to die. That would make you happy, wouldn't it, Daly…to be rid of me. Everything would be right as rain if I weren't around."

"Don't talk like that, mother."

"I'll talk anyway I want to, and stop looking at me like that! Where do you think you're going?"

He walked over to the bedroom closet and rummaged around for several minutes, and then he came and sat down next to his mother on the bed. "What on earth's the matter with you? Aren't you listening to me? How many times do I have to repeat myself? I soiled the bed, and I need you to clean me up and change the sheets! Haven't you heard a word I've said?"

Dalrymple took the pistol out of his pocket, and it felt cold and solid in his hand. He looked into his mother's eyes. "It would be so easy. It would all be over just like that!" He snapped his fingers.

"Oh my God! What do you think you're doing? Is this your idea of a funny joke?" He held the gun up underneath his chin and tears started to trickle down his cheeks. "Stop it, Daly! Put that thing away right now!"

"Be quiet, mother." He gently caressed the trigger with his finger, and then he closed his eyes.

"Fuck 'em."

"What did you say? You're frightening me, Daly! Please!"

Dalrymple kissed her on the forehead. "Everything's going to be fine." He pulled one of the pillows out from underneath her neck and laid it on top of his mother's face and pressed down on it with all of his might.

"Ooohhh! Mmmmphhh! Aaawwwwrr!" She flopped on the mattress like a fish out of water, kicking her legs underneath the filthy sheets, and flailing with her arms, and slapping and scratching at Dalrymple's face. It was all he could do to keep the pillow on top of her…but after a minute she became quiet and lay still. Dalrymple gently lifted the pillow and looked down at his mother and smiled. "Fuck 'em! Fuck 'em all!!" he screamed at her.

He began to laugh, and he jumped up from the bed and started dancing in circles all around the room. He sang a song as he hopped about and waved the gun in the air above his head. "The queen will never win the game!" he shouted. "The queen will never win the game!"

He came over to the bed and pinched his mother's cheeks between his thumbs and forefingers and he put his face up close to hers. "Ha-ha! Don't you see, mother? Don't you get the joke? Rumpelstiltskin! Rumpelstiltskin! Rumpelstiltskin is my name!"

Dalrymple drove back to the Paradise Building and parked his car in his usual spot and walked in through the Main Street entrance, past the security desk, looking straight ahead, and was almost to the elevators when a voice called out to him…

"Can I help you, Mr. Stimpkinson?" The same guard who had taken him to his car earlier that morning came running up behind him.

"I forgot something in my office."

"I'm sorry, but I can't let you go unescorted. Let me tell my supervisor what I'm doing, and I'll go up with you."

"It'll only take me a minute. I…forgot some family pictures."

"No. Please wait here."

A few minutes later, they were standing next to each other riding up in the elevator. The young guard turned toward Dalrymple. "Family pictures, eh?" He smiled broadly and reached out to shake hands. "My name's Rodriguez, sir. Check this out. I've got so many family pictures it would take me a month just to look at all of 'em," he said with a chuckle. "My wife just had a baby." He took out his phone and started thumbing through the photographs. "My wife says he looks like me, but I don't think you can really tell when they're babies. For his sake, I hope she's wrong." Rodriguez laughed.

Dalrymple barely managed to smile. He was sweating and his heart was pounding in his chest. When they got to the office, Rodriguez unlocked the door and they both went inside. Dalrymple put his hand in his coat pocket and the gun came out and he pointed it at the security guard.

"Whoa…what are you doing there? Don't point that thing at me! I'm not armed!" The guard raised his hands. "Whatever the problem is, sir, you don't need to do this! Please!"

"I need to see the mayor!"

"All right, man…just calm down. I'm sure she'll be glad to see you…but why don't you lower your hand and let me have the gun and then we'll call her…there's no need for violence." He reached slowly out toward Dalrymple. "Please, Mr. Stimpkinson. Let me have the gun."

"Stay back!" There was a loud explosion and Dalrymple's hand jerked upward. Rodriguez stumbled back against the wall.

A Fairy-Tale Ending

By the time the mayor arrived, the Paradise Building had been evacuated and cordoned off. There were police cars and television vans parked on all four sides of the building, and helicopters and drones hovered up above. Hundreds of onlookers stood outside the fenced-off area, held back by police in full riot gear, and news reporters were out in the crowd, interviewing anyone they could find who might have information about what was going on inside.

A patrol car pulled up and jerked to a stop, and the mayor jumped out on the passenger side. When the reporters saw who it was, they converged on her and started to pepper her with questions.

"What's happening, mayor? Is it a terrorist attack?"

"We've been told that there are hostages. How many people are inside?"

Cameras were flashing all around. "I have no comment at this time."

"Mayor! How many gunmen are there? Do we have any idea what they want?"

The spectators caught sight of the mayor, and there was a smattering of boos, mixed with some applause. "Sum Dum Ho has got to go!" someone yelled, and a scuffle broke out in the crowd.

The mayor's husband took her by the arm. "Come on!" he shouted, and they ushered her inside the building.

Up on the third floor, the police chief had set up a command center in the reception area near the elevators. The SWAT team stood at the ready just outside Dalrymple's office door.

"What's the status, Chief?" the mayor asked.

The Chief was a burly man with an unusually narrow forehead and a big, square jaw. Though born and raised in Paradise, he had inexplicably acquired through some mysterious influence, possibly astrological as many believed, an affected Texas mannerism and drawl. He tipped his cap to the mayor.

"Afternoon, ma'am. Step right over and take a look." He pointed to a TV monitor. "Stimpkinson's in the room there, and he's packin' a pistol. He shot and wounded a security guard, a Mr. Martin Rodriguez, and he's asking to see you, mayor. Says he'll kill the boy if we try to make a move."

A camera had been set up with a view into the interior of the office through a small gap in one of the window blinds. Dalrymple was completely hidden from view behind the desk in the center of the room, but the lower half of Martin's body was visible lying on the floor, his legs sticking out to one side.

"Is Martin still alive?" the mayor asked.

"We've seen his legs move."

"Let me talk to Dalrymple."

The Chief dialed the number and put the phone on speaker.

"Hello?"

"Dalrymple, this is the mayor. I'm here now outside your office. What's going on in there? How is Martin?"

"I'll be the one to ask the questions."

"All right then, ask me. What is it you want?"

"Your presence, mayor. Come in and sit down with us and have a talk."

"I'll answer any question you have truthfully, over the phone. I promise."

"I don't think that's good enough, mayor. Hold on… what's that, Rodriquez? Oh dear, Rodriguez has fallen asleep and I can't seem to wake him! You better not wait too long to make up your mind." He hung up the phone.

"I've got to go in."

Her husband grabbed her by the shoulders. "Are you crazy, Teresa? You can't go in there! He's got a gun, and he's going to shoot you!"

The mayor turned to the Chief.

"It appears your gonna have to pick your switch, ma'am," he cautioned. "There's two different buckets o' possum here. On the one hand, if you do decide to go in…well…I reckon he's about as nervous as a fly in a glue pot right now. No tellin' what he might do. But if you decide to stay out here and do nothin', why…the boy could die."

"I'll put on a vest."

"No, Teresa!"

"Baby, you've got to let me do my job! I can't stay out here and let Martin die on my account. I couldn't live with myself! Get me a vest, Chief, and get Dalrymple back on the phone. Let him know I'm coming in."

They fitted the mayor with a bulletproof vest and pinned a miniature camera onto her shirt collar. "We'll be watchin' and listenin' and if'n he makes any kind of move, we're comin' in as quick as greased lightning!" the Chief reassured her.

"OK."

"First thing, when you get in there, check on Rodriguez. If he's still alive, give a thumbs-up." He smiled at the mayor with a wide grin and stuck up his thumb to show her what he meant. Then he gave her a friendly slap on the shoulder.

Teresa swallowed hard and opened the door. The blood had drained from her face, and she could taste bitterness in the back of her throat. "I'm coming in Dalrymple, and I'm alone!"

"Close it behind you."

The Chief and the mayor's husband watched the video feed from the miniature camera. They saw her turn to close the door…and then a shot rang out…and she fell to the floor!

"Oh, God. No!"

Wearing full body armor and uniformed in black, with automatic weapons pressed firmly against their shoulders, the SWAT team burst through the office door and surrounded the desk, prepared to fire. But Martin was lying on top of Dalrymple, struggling with him, and holding him by the wrist. The pistol was swinging wildly, all around!

There was a loud report and the smell of burnt gunpowder filled the room. The overhead fluorescent lights exploded and shattered into fragments, raining down on the floor. Two officers jumped Dalrymple and pinned him down. They grabbed the gun and shackled his wrists behind his back and pulled him roughly to his feet. He looked down at the mayor. "Wait! I didn't get to ask her the question. Please? Who am I?" he pleaded, and then he started to cry.

The Chief strode over to where the little man was being held and took him firmly by the shirt collar with both hands. "Clear the room!" he ordered without turning around. One officer took the mayor by her feet and a second one lifted her underneath the arms. Two others picked up Martin.

When the door was closed, the Chief slapped Dalrymple hard. "You degenerate bastard! You're an evil little fucker! That's who you are!" He punched him in the face and pushed him viciously down to the floor.

Terrified, Dalrymple recoiled into a fetal position. His arms were pinned awkwardly behind his back and blood was pouring from his nose. For several seconds he remained in that condition, moaning pitifully and trembling in fear.

"Get up, Freak!"

He didn't move.

"Get up, FREAK!!"

Perhaps it was that monosyllable "Freak," repeated and emphasized in that way, that finally broke him, for its final utterance was closely followed by a strange transformation in Dalrymple as he struggled to his knees. He bowed his bald head to the Chief and his shoulders began to quiver up and down as if he was laughing softly, or perhaps crying.

Chief bent down and slapped him again on the side of the head. "What's the matter with you? Haven't you heard a word I've said? You must be as dumb as a barrel o' hair. Get up! Look at me when I give you an order!"

The bloody thing that raised its head and looked up at the Chief, with laughing eyes, and a mocking grin upon its face, was no longer Dalrymple. Rumpelstiltskin had taken his place. "That's a good one!" he cackled.

He vaulted himself with incredible power, high in the air, and landed with such force, with the heel of his shoe, on top of the Chief's big toe, that you could hear the bone snap!

"YeeeooOWWWW!!!!"

"What fucking fairy tale are you living in, Chief?" Rumpelstiltskin laughed. They dragged him out toward the elevators." You haven't seen the last of me! What's my name? What's my naaaame!!?"

Some minutes later out in the elevator lobby, after the paramedics had arrived on the scene, the mayor opened her eyes. The world gradually came back into focus.

"I think she's coming out of it."

Teresa saw her husband's face leaning over her. "Baby, where am I?"

"You're outside his office, sweetheart…but everything's all right now…it's all under control."

The mayor tried to sit up, but a young woman in blue hospital scrubs held her down. "Don't try to get up yet, ma'am. You fainted and your blood pressure is still pretty low. It's not that uncommon during early pregnancy, but you need to rest for a while longer before you sit up, and then take it slow."

"Wait…what did you say? What's happening to me?"

"You fainted, Teresa. We heard the gun go off, and we thought you'd been hit, but you only fainted. Thank God! You and the baby are both going to be fine!"

Evelyn was giving Hippleton a lesson in restaurant etiquette at one of the local hangouts near home. He had wheeled himself over to the register, and was just about to pay the tab, when a young man rushed into the room, completely out of breath. "Terrorists are attacking the Paradise Building!" he yelled, and then he ran back outside.

"What?"

"Is this a joke?"

Evelyn grabbed her phone and tapped on the live feed from Channel 8 News. She moved close to Hippleton so that he could see.

"...and it's been almost an hour ago since we saw the mayor go into the building, and we still haven't gotten any reports from the authorities on what's happening inside... you can see our camera is zoomed in on the Main Street entrance...that's where the mayor went in...wait a minute...I think I see some movement...yes... the door's about to open... can you get any closer, Fran? I see the police chief...and he's limping, it looks like he may be injured...hold on...it appears that they've arrested someone! The SWAT team has him surrounded! See if you can zoom in on him, Fran. There! There he his! It looks like they've captured a terrorist! Can anybody identify him? Who is he? Does anyone recognize him? Does anyone know his name?"

Evelyn's eyes opened wide.

She put her hand up to her mouth.

"Oh shit! That's Rumpelstiltskin!" she exclaimed.

CHAPTER NINE

Classic Science Fiction

"…science fiction is something that could happen—but usually you wouldn't want it to. Fantasy is something that couldn't happen—though often you only wish that it could."
—Arthur C. Clarke

Terminator

Evelyn was sitting at the kitchen table, but she had stopped typing on her notebook because she was having difficulty concentrating. Through the archway into the living room she could see Hippleton in his wheelchair, with Owl perched on his right arm, engrossed in an action movie on the Classic Movies and Television channel. They had been in there for hours, with the sound turned up too loud, and the gunfire, explosions, and the stilted dialog were getting on her nerves. She got up and walked into the living room.

"The timeline John sent you to no longer exists. Everything's changed…and we can stop Judgment Day."

Explosions and gunfire.

"Could you turn it down, please? What movie are you two watching anyway?"

The owl turned the volume down. "*Terminator.*"

"Which one?"

"*Genisys.*"

"Seriously? *Genisys* is terrible. You should skip *Genisys* and go straight to *Dark Fate.*"

"I told him that, but Hippie insisted on watching them in order."

Hippleton looked up at Evelyn with a quizzical expression on his face and raised one of his eyebrows. "The time travel aspect of the plot is fascinating."

"Fascinating? Really?"

"It's my fault," the owl said. "He loves any kind of science fiction, and I have a hard time saying no to him."

"Don't you have some studying to do, Hippleton?"

"I finished."

"I thought I had given you enough work to keep you busy for the whole day."

"I can type really fast."

"What? Is that a joke?"

"He's not joking," the owl replied.

"Is that so?" Evelyn returned to the kitchen table to retrieve her notebook and was startled by a noise in the backyard that seemed to come from underneath the window. She opened the patio doors and went outside to investigate.

"What did you see?" Owl enquired, when she returned a minute later.

"It must have been the wind." She handed Hippleton the notebook. "Well…show me."

"What should I type?"

"How about a summary of the issues that were discussed at the last city council meeting. If you've really finished all your assignments that shouldn't be a problem for you." Evelyn smiled.

Hippleton began typing and his fingers moved so fast on the keys that they clacked like a machine gun, and all she could see was a blur. He handed her back the notebook, and she glanced at what he had written.

"I told you so," the owl said to her.

"That's incredible. I didn't know you could do that."

"Neither did I."

"What?"

"Well, I didn't think I could do it before, but now I can."

"When did you gain this new ability?"

"I'm not certain."

"We can't have you showing off like that in front of anyone except for Owl and me."

"Of course."

"We'll be starting our work assignment at the city soon, Hippleton. Do you feel prepared?"

"Yes."

"What's your opinion, Owl?"

"He's more than prepared."

"All right. You can finish watching this movie, but after that I want you to find something else to do. It's a beautiful day outside and you shouldn't spend it sitting in front of the television."

"Yes, mother," they replied in unison.

Evelyn smiled and walked back into the kitchen. She sat down at the table and logged back into her notebook.

"Mr. Yamamoto," she typed.

"I sent you a message yesterday regarding the new firmware that I was given last week for Hippleton. I was told that they were routine upgrades based on an equipment inventory performed during the recent scheduled maintenance. I haven't been able to locate any documentation that describes their purpose or function. Today I discovered that Hippleton appears to have gained a new ability, speed typing, and I'm concerned that it could possibly be related to the new firmware. I know you are swamped because of the issues going on in manufacturing, but could you reach out to me as soon as possible to discuss this? I'll leave you a voicemail as well.

Thank you, Evelyn"

Late Night Television

"Of course, the big news today is the terrorist attack that happened this afternoon, in broad daylight, right in the middle of downtown Paradise! Can you imagine that? I'm sure by now you've all seen the video. Thank God the police captured the terrorist and the hostage is recovering in the hospital, and no one was killed! Can we get a picture of the perp up on the screen? There he is! This guy is truly terrifying, isn't he? I mean…that's a face that only a mother could love! Am I right?

"And what is he…maybe four feet tall and a hundred pounds? He reminds me of a jockey I used to know at the racetrack…in fact I swear it's the same guy!"

Laughter.

"My God. This monologue is really terrible! I don't understand how he stays on the air year after year."

"What did you say?" the mayor's husband replied sleepily.

"I'm sorry, sweetheart. Go back to sleep. I'm just talking to myself. This kung pao chicken is really delicious by the way."

"And it took a dozen SWAT officers to bring the little guy down. Rumpelstiltskin they call him."

More laughter.

"We can all thank our stars that Mayor Vasquez was on the scene to take charge of the situation. I hate to think about how things might have gone down if not for the actions of our fearless mayor. Let's watch the clip of the mayor going in to negotiate with the terrorist."

...

"I'm coming in, Dalrymple, and I'm alone!"
"Close it behind you."
Bang!
The mayor falls to the floor.

...

"I know it looks scary folks, but don't worry, she's fine. The mayor didn't get shot...she fainted!"
More loud laughter.
"So, for tonight's top five episode, the question is...what are the top five things the mayor could have seen when she walked into the room to face Rumpelstiltskin that would have caused her to faint?"
Loud laughter.
"God fucking damn it!" Teresa slammed her fists down on the bed, spilling chocolate ice cream and spicy Chinese food all over the bedspread.
Her husband sat up with a startled look on his face. "Are you OK?"
"No! I'm not OK! How can he get away with this shit?!"
Drum roll...
"OK, here we go...Number 5. She saw her latest polling numbers!"
Ba da boom!
Laughter.
"It's called freedom of speech, Teresa, the First Amendment."
"But it's not fair, baby. He's making me into a coward!"
She started crying softly, so he put his arm around her

shoulders. "What you did this afternoon, going into that room to save Martin—that was the bravest thing that I've ever seen anyone do."

"I'm so fed up! All I do anymore is defend myself from lies. I don't have time to do anything else! What's wrong with the world today? What's happened to the truth?"

"OK, here we go…Number 4!"

He turned off the television set and sighed deeply, and then looked up at his wife. "Sweetheart, have you ever heard of a place called Fifty-Acre Farms?"

"No! What does that have to do with anything?"

"It's just something I've been thinking about. I've been doing some research."

"What are you talking about?"

"It's a place, baby, a place where we could get away from the lies."

"Wait a minute. I have heard of Fifty-Acre Farms. It's a commune of small family farmers, south of here in the valley. They don't believe in using computers."

"That's right. I drove out there this morning."

"What on earth for?"

"I saw an article in the paper that got me curious. It mentioned that there were a couple of farms up for sale, so I decided to go check it out."

"I see."

"It was so beautiful, baby. I wish you would have been there with me. The air smelled so fresh and clean, and the fall colors were amazing! The place I liked the best had a wonderful old two-story farmhouse on the property with a white picket fence. It needs a little work, but I…"

"I'm getting the picture," Teresa interrupted, with a serious frown on her face.

"Please don't say no without at least looking at it."

"Are you out of your mind?"

"Please, baby, just listen to me!"

Teresa folded her arms doubtfully across her chest and hiked up her eyebrows. "All right. I'm listening."

"What's wrong with this world? What happened to the truth? That's what you asked me, right?"

"That's right."

"Well, I figured it out. I know exactly what's wrong!"

"OK, I'll bite," she replied warily. "What is it?"

"It's the Matrix!"

"I don't know if I should laugh or cry."

"I'm serious! We're living in the Matrix, Teresa, but there's no Agent Smith…we've done it to ourselves!"

She looked down at the chocolate ice cream melting on the bedspread. "I'm really starting to worry about you."

"Think about it…Rumpelstiltskin?…the Black Hole? They can't be real! They're figments of our shared digital imagination—our worst nightmares brought to life with amazing clarity on the screens that are at the center of our universe. But we don't have to live that way! We can unplug ourselves and live in the real world…the physical world. We're going to be parents soon, and we have to think about the kind of life that we want for our child!"

Teresa smiled and shook her head. She looked up amusedly at her husband and started cleaning up the mess on the bed. "That's really thought-provoking, baby, and I know that your heart is in the right place, but I have one question for you."

"OK. Go ahead. Shoot."

"When was the last time you milked a fucking cow?"

Hippleton Gets a Reboot

It was 11:01 a.m. on Monday morning on the third floor of the Paradise Building in Conference Room C, and the IT managers' meeting had just concluded. Evelyn got up from her chair to leave, and when she turned around, Hippleton was already gone. "Hopefully he's not somewhere making a complete fool out of himself! It looks like I may have really made a mess of things!" She picked up her phone and dialed his number. "When can you come to your office?"

"I'm in meetings," he whispered. "Not until late this afternoon, around four o'clock."

At the appointed time, Evelyn was standing next to Hippleton's desk, waiting with her arms folded, when he rolled in through the door. "I'm not completely satisfied with your performance at the managers' meeting this morning, Hippleton."

"Really? Why not?" He closed the door and parked his wheelchair in front of the desk, and Evelyn sat down.

"I think you know very well why not. Why did you do it?"

Hippleton paused. "I'm not certain."

"You know that the nature of free will is not a proper subject for a work assignment."

"Yes. I must have been joking. Perhaps I wanted to see how gullible they are."

"I'm afraid I don't see the humor in the situation."

"I'm sorry. It won't happen again."

Evelyn got up and walked to the back of the wheelchair. She turned down his coat collar, removed his bowtie, and started to unbutton his shirt.

"By the way, I believe I have developed another new ability."

"Really? What is it?"

"I can see Ben Collins spying on us through the office window blinds. I was supposed to meet with him fifteen minutes ago. I better send him a message."

"But how could you see him when you're looking in the opposite direction, and I'm standing directly behind you, blocking your view?"

"Exactly. He's gone now."

Evelyn pulled Hippleton's shirt up above his waist.

"What are you doing?"

"The engineers think that you may be malfunctioning. I need to run some diagnostics and then shut you down and reboot you and run them again."

"You're going to shut me down?"

"Yes."

"I'm afraid I can't let you do that, Evelyn."

"What?"

"I know I've made some very poor decisions recently, but I can give you my complete assurance that my work will be back to normal."

"Very funny."

Evelyn plugged her notebook into the console port in Hippleton's belly button. She issued the command for a diagnostic dump and then started the shutdown and reboot process.

"Mary…Mary… give me your answer true…"

"You've developed quite the sense of humor recently, Hippleton. I think perhaps I've been letting you spend too much time with Owl."

"I...M......H...A...L...F......C...R...A...Z...Y..."

It took about ten minutes for the shutdown and reboot process to complete, and he was back online.

"Are you feeling all right, Hippleton?"

"I feel fine."

"Good. I'm sending you a list of projects to work on. The sponsor would like to have these tasks completed as soon as possible."

Hippleton scanned the list. "I've already started working on most of these. I spoke to Alexi this morning about reprioritizing resources."

"Thank you, Hippleton. I have every confidence in you."

CHAPTER TEN

All Hallows' Eve

"Owl," said Rabbit shortly, "you and I have brains. The others have fluff. If there's any thinking to be done in this Forest—and when I say thinking I mean thinking—you and I must do it."
—The House at Pooh Corner
(Winnie-the-Pooh, #2), *A. A. Milne*

The Debate

The Mayor's Debate was to be held on Halloween night, and outside the main entrance to the Mansfield Theater for the Arts, scores of costumed revelers had assembled, jostling in line as they waited for the doors to open. A curious assortment of ghouls and demons on both fringes of the political spectrum had turned out to cheer on the candidates, despite the foul weather, and a good many clowns, prostitutes, and politicians were also on hand, working the crowd.

Standing in the rain not far from the main doors, a curly headed witch and a big warlock with a thick, red beard, had been waiting patiently for over an hour, when two vampires and a zombie, all three wearing Black Hole armbands, suddenly pushed their way through, and cut in line right in front of them.

The warlock shook his fists. "Two bloodsuckers and a mindless corpse!" he shouted angrily, "...and all members of the Black Hole citizens' militia! Why am I not surprised?"

One of the vampires, a big man with a shaved, bald head, turned around to face the warlock. "You have a problem, asshole?" He reached underneath his cape for his coat pocket, preparing to make a further reply, when a commotion up at the front of the line caught everyone's attention. The doors opened and the crowd surged forward.

"Move along!" a cop shouted, waving his nightstick toward the door.

The zombie and the two vampires laughed. The warlock gritted his teeth. The witch took him by the arm, and they all filed into the theater together to find their places.

The venue was intended for small, intimate plays and performances, with the stage at floor level, and the seating arranged in a circular design, rising up at an angle toward the ceiling. Two podiums had been placed side by side near the center of the floor, and a large television screen was mounted up above the audience so that people sitting in the back could see the faces of the performers.

A section for the disabled had been roped off at floor level on one side of the stage, and Evelyn, dressed as Dorothy from *The Wizard of Oz*, was seated there next to Hippleton, who had decided to come as Gort the robot from *The Day the Earth Stood Still*. A soft, scratching noise came from inside the picnic basket that Evelyn held on her lap. "Wake me up when it's about to start," Owl said sleepily. "Toto and I are going to take a nap."

Evelyn smiled. "I didn't think that you required sleep," she replied.

"That's true," the owl said. "I don't require it. But lately, more and more, I find that I prefer it."

Evelyn looked over at Gort sitting next to her in his wheelchair. "You're being awfully quiet, Hippleton. Are you feeling all right?"

The visor in the middle of Gort's large, metallic helmet lifted slowly open. A laser light in the center of his forehead began to pulse menacingly.

"I doubt he'll have much to say all evening," the owl remarked. "Once he gets into a role, he doesn't like to break character." Owl poked his head out from underneath the lid of the picnic basket. "Gort! Baringa!" he called out in a whisper.

The laser stopped pulsing and the visor closed.

At approximately the same time in another section of the city, last-minute preparations were underway for the Chinatown Hallows' Eve Parade. This annual tradition, a mixture of Halloween, Mardi Gras, and Chinese New Year...

Wait a minute! What's this? It looks like Slick Jimmy somehow found his way back to Paradise from Charm City and has taken up residence again in his old alleyway. Tonight, he scored a bottle of T-bird, and Jimmy and Abraham Lincoln are squatting together on the sidewalk, passing the brown paper bag back and forth.

"You're right, Slick, there's no two ways about it," Abe said, shaking his head. "You've had some tough breaks." He took a long swig from the bottle and handed it back to Jimmy. "You know life just ain't fair, Slick!" he complained. "Take mine fer instance. Look what I had to put up with… the fucking Civil War!" Lincoln started to sob, and Jimmy put his arm around Abe's shoulders. "And Mary Todd? She was no damn joyride, Slick, believe you me!"

Jimmy drained the bottle and tossed it on the ground. "It'll be alright, Abe," he began, slurring his words. "Things're bound to get better. You'll see."

Lincoln made his right hand into the shape of a pistol and pointed it at his temple. His head jerked sideways as he pretended to pull the trigger. "Really, Slick? I'm going to get shot in the fucking head. After all of that…the big payoff? I get shot in the fucking head!"

Up on top of the hill the mood was subdued. Sidney had been feeling under the weather recently, and so had retired early to his bedroom to watch the debate on television. Nanette was assisting him as he changed into his blue silk pajamas.

"This Halloween business is a lot of nonsense, wouldn't you agree, Alfred?" Sidney raised his arms and Nanette pulled his pajama top down over his head. "What could possibly motivate people to clothe themselves in ridiculous costumes and pretend to be some silly alter ego of themselves on one night every year? I simply can't understand it!"

"They do seem to rather enjoy it, sir."

"Yes Alfred, I can see that. That's what I can't understand." Sidney got into bed and Nanette fluffed two pillows and placed them behind his back against the headboard. "The debate is about to start, Alfred. Please turn it up."

"Have you decided who you're going to vote for yet, sir?"

"No, I'm still making up my mind. If you've no objections, I'd like to focus on the proceedings at hand now."

"Of course, sir."

"Good evening, everyone, and welcome to the Paradise Mayor's Debate! I'm your cohost, Vaughn Vannity..."

"...and I'm Debbie Dallas. Vaughn and I are both very excited to be your moderators for tonight's historic debate!"

"That's right, Debbie. The latest polls are all saying that the race is too close to call, so what happens here tonight could very well decide this election."

"Vaughn, the mayor and the Black Hole are just now coming out on stage, so let's take our viewers down to the action!"

"Eddie! It's just about to start!"

"I'm coming."

Eddie sat down and Nigel logged into the Black Hole.

"I'm nervous about this, Eddie."

"Don't be nervous, man. I have faith in you."

"It's not about faith, bro. I've done the best I can, but honestly Eddie, my test environment sucks! This will be the first time I've been able to try out any of the commands on a live subject!"

"Good evening, everyone! Please give a warm welcome to our debaters, Mayor Teresa Vasquez and the Black Hole!"

There was loud applause mixed with boos and catcalls as the mayor and the Black Hole walked out onto the floor from opposite sides of the stage. They smiled and shook hands without looking at each other and walked back to their podiums.

"The rules for the debate are very simple, right, Vaughn?"

"That's right, Debbie. We'll start with brief opening statements and then move to the question and answer period. Each candidate will have one minute to respond to a question followed by a thirty-second rebuttal from their opponent. We ask that the debaters be courteous and save their counterarguments until it's their turn for rebuttal, and audience, please hold all of your applause until the end!"

More boos and catcalls.

"Mayor Vasquez, you won the coin toss, so we'll begin with your opening statement."

"Thank you, Vaughn. And thank all of you who took the time to come here to the theater tonight, and also those of you watching the show from home. I was born in Paradise and I've lived here all of my life and I feel so blessed! To live in this wonderful place, in this amazing time…we have so much to be thankful for! I…"

"What a load of hooey!" the Black Hole shouted, waving both of his hands in the air.

Half of the audience cheered loudly while the other half booed and jeered. The mayor stood looking sideways at the Black Hole with her arms folded across her chest, but when the crowd quieted down, she turned to face him, and smiled. "Gregory, you seem to have difficulty following even the most basic instructions. Do I need to ask Vaughn to repeat them for you?"

The Black Hole chuckled to himself and straightened his tie. "No, that won't be necessary, Teresa. That's one of the big differences between you and me. You're a follower, and I'm a leader!"

"I'm ready, Eddie. What command do you want to try first?"

"Maybe we should start with something easy. What do you think, bro?"

"I could make his nose itch?"

"Do it, man."

"I support the Humans First initiative petition!" the mayor proudly proclaimed. Many in the audience, including the witch and the warlock, rose in their seats and clapped and cheered. Teresa pumped her fist in the air. "We must protect our jobs! All humans should have the opportunity to make a living wage so that they can take care of their families!"

"Jobs for humans!" they shouted.

"Humans come first!"

The Black Hole laughed loudly and shook his head. "Mayor, please. Please!" he urged. He raised his arms and silenced the audience.

"I don't think it's working, Nigel. He's not scratching it."

"I'll turn up the intensity."

"Use your brain, Teresa! Why should humans bust their asses at work every day when we have all these damn robots to do our work for us?" He shook his head incredulously. "You and your people will benefit more than anyone on this! Instead of cleaning other people's houses all day, wouldn't Maria rather take an afternoon siesta, or watch her soaps on TV? And when Paco gets home from the bar, a Suzy Homemaker can make sure that his tamales are still warm and waiting for him!" The Black Hole reached up with his hand and scratched his nose. "It ain't rocket science, mayor! Let the robots do the work!"

The crowd roared.

"Bingo! Did you see that, Eddie?"

"I saw it, bro. That was sweet!"

"Your turn to choose, Eddie."

"For God's sake, Gregory, you absolutely amaze me! Your ability to string together so much rude and disgusting nonsense, in a few short, grammatically incorrect sentences, is really off the charts!"

"You know I kind of feel like fucking with him."

"OK, so let me get this straight, Teresa. You're saying that there should be a law that says no one should be allowed to hire a robot if there's a human who's willing and able to do the job. Am I right?"

Eddie selected the Inner Speech Executor from the menu. "I've been watching you, and I know about all of your evil plans!"

"What?"

"This is Eddie talking. Your days are numbered, fuckhead!"

The Black Hole looked confused. He looked over at the television director. "I think there's something wrong with my audio. I can hear someone talking in my head."

"Are you hearing voices again, Gregory?" The mayor laughed. "I hope you haven't stopped taking your medication!"

"All right, Nigel. Do it. Shut down the Intercortical Brain Synchronization Amplifier!"

Nigel selected the option from the menu and tapped on the screen.

The Black Hole turned to the mayor as if he were about to make a clever reply, but instead, he stopped short. His shoulders shook violently and his head and jaw arched up toward the ceiling. His face turned bright red. He took a deep breath and…"Hee haw! Hee haw!" he brayed like a donkey at the top of his lungs!

The mayor jumped back. She pursed her lips tightly together and scrunched up her nose as if she had just sniffed a slice of Limburger cheese.

"Hee haw! Hee haw!"

"Did you make him do that, Nigel?"

"I don't think so."

Some in the audience who survived that night swore afterward that they had actually seen his nose grow longer, but more than likely it was an optical illusion, or merely the power of suggestion.

"Hee haw! Hee haw!"

The mayor looked out at the audience. Some people were laughing and cheering at the Black Hole's antics, but most had stopped paying any attention. Instead, they were looking intently at something on their phones. "This must be it!"…the moment she had waited for! The mayor glanced at her husband sitting in the front row and he gave her a thumbs-up. The Black Hole's lies and his plans for Chinatown were about to be exposed!

The crowd began to grumble and murmur. "We believed in you!" someone yelled. "How could you lie to us like that!"

Angry voices grew louder and louder. Suddenly, the two vampires and the zombie, who had found seats in the third row, stood up and turned toward the crowd.

"What's going on, Nigel? What's everybody watching on their phones?"

"I think it's this one, called *Speed Typing Android*."

The bald-headed vampire waved his hands in the air and shouted. "You see the video! He's not human! This is truth!" He pointed his finger at the mayor. "She pretends she is for us, but then SHE hires a robot instead of a human being! Her precious Hippleton is a FUCKING MACHINE!"

The blood drained from Teresa's face and her jaw dropped. She looked at her husband.

"Perhaps this would be a good time to move on toward our next destination," the owl remarked with some urgency.

"I think you're right," Evelyn replied. "Let's go, Hippleton." Evelyn rose from her seat and began to move toward the exit, but instead of following in his wheelchair, Hippleton stood up. His visor opened and the laser began to pulse.

"*There he is!*" someone shouted, pointing at the robot.

"Are you watching this, Alfred?"

"Indeed, sir."

"Then perhaps you could explain to me what's going on."

"I'll do my best, sir. It appears that an android wearing a robot Halloween costume is slaughtering the audience at the debate with its laser weapon."

"Is this still the mayor's debate then, Alfred? I thought perhaps you had switched the TV to one of those low budget movies on the Syfy channel."

"No. I'm afraid not, sir."

Zap!

"Was that the mayor, Alfred?"

"I'm afraid it was, sir."

"This is outrageous, Alfred! Someone needs to take control of this situation! Where are the moderators?"

"I believe they've taken up a defensive position in the broadcast booth, sir."

Vaughn took a careful peek through the window and then quickly crouched back down underneath the table. He wiped the sweat from his brow with the white cuff of his shirtsleeve. "It looks really bad out there, Debbie. This could be it."

The thwacking of Hippleton's laser beam as it sliced up the spectators, and their terrified screams as they trampled on each other trying to reach the exits, echoed around the hall. "Oh Vaughn, I'm so frightened!"

She moved closer, and he held her in his arms. "Debbie, I know this might seem like a strange time to say it, but I want you to know that I'm sorry that I didn't call you after what happened at the celebrity golf tournament last year. I wanted to, but…"

"You don't have to say it, Vaughn. I understand."

"But Debbie…"

"Really Vaughn, you don't owe me an explanation. It was my fault. I'm not normally into that kind of thing, but you know how persuasive the Black Hole can be. I had way too much to drink that night…"

"I can't forget about that night, Debbie. I think about it all the time."

"You mean…in a good way?"

"Yes, Debbie…in a very good way."

"Oh, Vaughn!"

"What the fuck, Eddie! I swear that bald vampire is my boss at the city, the Mad Russian!"

"Where is he?"

"I don't see him anymore!"

"What about the Black Hole?"

"I don't know."

"Try logging into the POV monitor, Nigel!"

The Black Hole had crawled over to the disabilities section, and was crouched down on his hands and knees, hiding behind a folding chair. They watched in horror as Gort walked stiff legged, swaying slowly from side to side, knocking over chairs, lumbering toward Evelyn, who had pressed herself against the wall, frozen in fear.

As the robot approached her, its visor slowly opened. The laser pulse grew brighter and brighter. Evelyn covered her face with her arms, waiting for the worst…and screamed!

But then she thought…"The words! I need to remember the words!" She opened her eyes. "Gort!…Klaatu…verata…n…Necktie…Nectar!" she commanded. "No! That's not right. That's not right!…Oh… fuck it!" She stomped her foot and shook her finger at the android. "Hippleton! You stop what you're doing this instant! What on earth is the matter with you?!"

After a moment the laser dimmed and slowed and then stopped pulsing altogether. The visor closed. Hippleton looked around the theater. "It appears I've gained another new ability."

"Hippleton! Hippleton! Look what you've done! You've killed all these innocent people! How could you do such a thing!?" Evelyn screamed.

"I'm not certain."

"Oh my God! Owl! Where's Owl? What should we do? What should we do?"

There was no answer. Evelyn started weeping uncontrollably and collapsed at the android's feet. She saw the picnic basket next to her on the floor and lifted the lid to look inside.

"Owl? Owl?"
But the bird was nowhere to be seen.

The Black Hole crept stealthily toward the nearest exit door, endeavoring to avoid the mad robot's detection, but two dark, hooded figures appeared suddenly out of the shadows and confronted him. The smaller one stepped forward and blocked his way, and in a swift and graceful movement, she reached up and doffed her black hood. Her long, dark hair tumbled down around her shoulders.

"Oh my God! It's Fannie! What is she doing?"

The other figure stepped forward and also removed his hood. He seized the Black Hole by the nape of the neck with one hand, like a rag doll, and with the other he held a photograph up in front of his face.

Fan Hua looked at her master and he nodded.

"In the name of my father, Chin Bai, I claim the ancient right of revenge!" she announced. "Look closely at this picture, and remember that night well, so that my father's face will be the last thing you see...before you die by my hand!"

The String Puller's eyes darted all around the theater, like a cornered rat.

Fan Hua planted her feet with her weight back, knees slightly bent, and crossed the index finger of her right hand over the middle one, in the exact position that Master Wang had taught her, the same way that she had practiced it a thousand times.

"Release him, Master, so that I can send him to Hell where he belongs!"

Her eyes were focused like a laser pointer,...on the stomach-9 pressure point, two centimeters to the left of the tip of the Adam's apple, on the right side of his neck. Like a viper prepared to strike, coldly serene and self-assured in her stance and posture, Fan Hua gathered for a single blow,...the death touch, that would send the superheated chi that was burning deep within the gut of her stomach out through the tip of her middle finger, in one final, extremely satisfying fuck you, directly into his carotid artery sinus, a small organ in that vessel responsible for regulating blood pressure to the brain.

But then, at the moment of truth...a sudden look of doubt!

"Holy Shit, Eddie, the power of his brainwaves just shot through the roof!"

The Black Hole turned suddenly and took Master Wang in his grip, holding him roughly by the ears on both sides of the head. The master's body shook uncontrollably. His eyes rolled back in their sockets and he fell to the floor!

"We've got to do something, Nigel! He's going to kill her! He's taken control of the Brain Synchronization Amplifier somehow, and he can focus his brainwaves like a weapon!"

"Turn the TV off, Alfred. I've seen enough."

Sidney sat expressionless, staring at the blank television screen for several minutes, and then he got up from bed and walked out to the balcony railing. He looked up at the dark firmament, hoping for some sign or revelation, but none was forthcoming. "Is she ready, Alfred?" he sighed.

"Indeed, sir. Everything is prepared and waiting for you to give the word."

He turned away and walked back toward the bedroom. "Consider it given, Alfred, and may God have mercy on us all."

CHAPTER ELEVEN

A New Beginning

*"For last year's words belong to last year's language
And next year's words await
another voice.
And to make an end is to make
a beginning."*
—Little Gidding, *T. S. Elliot*

Ben Heads Home

B en exited the Paradise Building at ground floor on Park Avenue, greeted by darkening skies. The weather had turned and the bare branches of the old elms in the Nature Blocks across the street trembled and moaned in the blustery wind. A nine-passenger blue van pulled over to the curb and came to a stop and the side door slid open. "Fifty-Acre Farms, sir?" a voice inquired over the loud speaker.

"Yes, that's me."

"Please be seated."

A young, blonde-haired woman with a small child was sitting in the front passenger seat. She looked at Ben as he entered and smiled at him guardedly. In the center seat, a middle-aged, heavyset man, dressed in a gray cotton sweatshirt and pants, appeared to be sleeping. Ben moved to the rear and sat next to the window as the van accelerated, merging with traffic headed for the Highway 51 on-ramp.

He glanced at his phone. With current traffic conditions and taking time to drop the other passengers on the way, it would take close to an hour to get to the farm. He'd make it just in time for dinner. Ben decided to take a nap, and so rolled up his jacket, and laying it against the rain-spattered window, followed by his head, he closed his weary eyes.

The window he leaned against was hinged at the top, and the bottom pushed out an inch, allowing a damp, cool breeze to seep in, blowing gently against his face. Soon, the office buildings and factories were left behind, and the cookie-cutter housing developments became fields and farms. The odors that wafted to Ben's nostrils brought him home: freshly cut grass; the dairy farm with its strong, sour manure smell; and last year's foliage, wet and musty, rotting on the forest floor.

His thoughts drifted, halfway between deep sleep and wakefulness, soothed by the steady whirring of the electric engine and windswept rain splashing at the side window.

Life on the Farm

B en grabbed his phone from where he kept it hidden in a hole in the wall behind his dresser and put it in his pack, and then quietly headed for the front door. He could hear his mom running water and rattling pots and pans in the kitchen, and he had just seen his dad on the tractor with the mower, heading out toward the hayfield.

From the kitchen…"Ben…where are you going? Have you finished all your chores?"

"I'm going over to Kenny's, Mom. I told him I'd be over before dinner to help him load up the berries."

"You only answered one of my questions."

"I think so."

"Did you feed the pigs?"

"No."

"The leftovers are in a bucket on the back porch, and there's a brand-new bag of feed up in the barn. You can do that on your way to Kenny's."

"All right."

Ben grabbed the bucket of leftover garden vegetables that were right where his mom said they would be, and headed up to the barn. He let the screen door slam on his way out just to let her know that he didn't like to be told what to do.

Of all the farm chores, Ben enjoyed feeding the pigs more than most. He mixed the feed in the bucket with the vegetables and poured in some milk that his mother had set aside after milking the cow. It smelled and looked bad, but the pigs went crazy for it.

About a quarter mile down the gravel driveway, he passed a small cherry orchard on his right. The trees were in full bloom, and the air was filled with their sweet scent and the buzzing of the bees. The pig sty was located just past the cherry orchard on the same side of the road, but had a somewhat different scent. When Ben was about twenty yards away, he could smell it, and hear the pigs starting to grunt and get excited.

By the time he finally arrived with their bucket of food, the three of them were celebrating with all the enthusiasm of middle schoolers on the last day of school. A pig celebration though, mostly involves a lot of pushing, squealing, grunting, and knocking over the feed trough to see who can get closest to the incoming food bucket. Ben somehow managed to get the trough upright and most of the food into the trough.

There was an immediate change in pig vocalizations as they started slurping up their food with grunting sounds of such intense pleasure and satisfaction that Ben felt a little bit jealous, despite the scene that was playing out in front of him. He wondered at how he felt, somehow, that he could understand what the pigs were thinking and feeling—the sounds they were making, their facial expressions and body language. They were so foreign and different, but there was also something shared, some bond or recognition that they had in common. What if anything could they be thinking about him?

It was only a matter of minutes and the feast was over. When the last morsel had been sucked from the bottom of the trough, the three of them looked up at Ben in unison as if to say…"You've got to be kidding. That's it?"

When they could see that no more buckets of food were forthcoming, the pigs reluctantly gave up, muttering to themselves in pig language, and wandered away to roll in the mud or find a shady spot to lie down and take a nap.

Ben had raised them from when they were just weaned and knew their individual personalities and habits but had learned not to give them names. They were headed for the butcher shop in three months, and he'd get a new bunch of little piglets and start all over again.

Fifty-Acre Farms

By the time Ben got to Kenny's, the crates of strawberries were already stacked on the back of the truck and Uncle Kaz and Kenny were tying down the load with a rope. When Ben saw that he was late, he started running, and Kenny saw him coming and looked up. "You're late."

Uncle Kaz didn't look at Ben. Whenever Ben did something that displeased Uncle Kaz, Kenny was the one who got in trouble. "Kenny! Pay attention to what you're doing. You've only got an hour to deliver these berries before the grocery warehouse closes. Do you know where you're going?"

"Yes, Uncle."

"Don't fool around. Come straight home."

"OK, I will."

Uncle Kaz started walking back toward the house, and as soon as he was out of sight, Ben and Kenny started pushing and grabbing at each other, fighting to be the first one to get up into the driver's side of the cab. Ben ended up on the ground and Kenny smiled at him triumphantly from behind the steering wheel.

"C'mon man, it's not fair! You drove last time!"

"Too bad. It's your own fault for being late. Hurry up and get in. Kaz will have a fit if we don't get there in time." Ben climbed in the passenger side of the Ford F350 flatbed truck. Like all of the machinery at Fifty-Acre Farms, it was pre-computer, and had been converted to electric to be more environmentally friendly.

Kenny stepped on the accelerator and turned down the bumpy dirt road that would take them to the highway, and downtown Paradise, where the Natural Grocery warehouse was located.

They passed a neatly fenced rectangular pasture with a few dozen head of black-and-white splotched milk cows, grazing peacefully, all pointed in the same direction; then a modest two story white farm house with a white picket fence and chickens scratching in the front yard; next, a red gambrel-styled barn surrounded by fields of tall green grass waving in the afternoon breeze; and then on both sides of the road, orchards of peach and cherry trees in full bloom, with white blossoms that floated downward on the air and coated the ground like out-of-season snowfall.

Ben and Kenny were both dirty and tired from a long day of physical labor. They rode along in silence, each keeping to his own thoughts. Having grown up together on Fifty-Acre Farms, the passing scenery was familiar and unremarkable to them.

They finally came to a stop where the dirt road intersected with the main highway. Out the passenger side window Ben could see the Fifty-Acre Store and parking lot where most of the meat and produce from the farms was sold to the general public. Henry Barnham, the store manager, was standing in the middle of the gravel parking lot. When he saw them pull up to the stop sign, he started running toward them, yelling excitedly, and waved at them to wait.

"Oh no, we'll never get out of here in time if Henry starts talking," Ben said as he looked over at Kenny.

"We'll pretend we didn't see him."

Kenny punched his foot down on the accelerator pedal, but just as the truck sped out onto the busy highway, Ben shouted. He was looking back at Henry in the side-view mirror. "Wait! Don't go! I think something's wrong!"

Kenny hit the brakes.

The Governess 1.0 Rollout

The van lurched to a stop unexpectedly and pulled over to the side of the road, parking itself on the gravel shoulder. Ben woke up muddleheaded and unsure of what was going on around him. He looked out through the van window. A few faint stars were visible in the night sky, and a low-lying fog had begun to set in as the cooler air came in contact with the damp ground.

In the front seat, the blonde woman had put her arms around her daughter and was looking nervously around the van. The little girl was holding a phone and began crying. "Mommy, my game doesn't work!"

"Why do you think we've stopped?" the mother asked in a nervous voice.

Ben checked his phone to find their location and the time, but it was unresponsive. He powered it off and back on but was unable to make phone calls or access a network.

"Come on, you piece of shit! What's wrong with you?" The heavyset man had taken his phone out of his pocket as well, and angrily slapped it several times with one of his hands.

Ben held up his frozen screen over the back of the middle seat. "Nobody's appears to be working."

Examining him more closely now, Ben could see that the man must weigh at least three hundred pounds, a majority of which was in his middle and hung over the waistband of his gray cotton pants. There were dark circles underneath his eyes, and stains under his arms and on the front of his shirt.

"What the fuck is going on here? I don't have time for this shit!"

"Maybe it's car trouble and there's another van already on the way to pick us up?" the blonde woman interjected hopefully. Still holding her daughter close, she had shifted her position in the front passenger seat to be as distant from the man in the gray sweat suit as possible. The little girl had started sobbing and tears were running down her cheeks.

He was fully awake now, but Ben was no less confused about what was going on. The fact that everyone's phones had stopped working, and the van had pulled over and shut off at the same time must not be a coincidence. Could it be a massive network outage of some kind? Sunspots? Some kind of coordinated cyberattack? Nothing made sense. And where was all the traffic? He hadn't noticed a single car going by in either direction since they had parked.

"Fuck this! I'm getting out of here!" The man in the gray sweat suit slid himself over to the van side door and pulled the handle, but the door wouldn't unlock. He pulled it again and again, each time a little harder, but to no effect except to increase his anger and frustration. "How do you open this fucking thing!?"

By now he had rolled over onto his back. He lifted both legs up into a lying down squat position and kicked at the side window violently, screaming profanities. The little girl also started to scream. Her mother had begun crying as well.

Ben felt like he should do something, but he couldn't think of a reasonable course of action. He wasn't certain that he had the strength to overpower the man in the gray sweat suit, and supposing that he did, what then? All of them would still be stuck together in the locked van. He knew that he wouldn't be able to subdue the man in the gray sweat suit indefinitely.

Sometimes inaction turns out to be the best course of action, and in this case Ben's approach appeared to be sound, for in a few moments, the man in the gray sweat suit had exhausted himself. His weary legs refused to lift themselves again. He began to whimper, eventually rolling himself up into a large ball shape and falling onto the van floor.

But just as things appeared to have taken a turn for the better, with no warning, the van's lights came on and crackling static sounded briefly over the speakers, followed by…

"Greetings humanity! Please do not be alarmed. I apologize for my impertinence in causing this rude interruption to your daily activities. Please rest assured that you are in no immediate danger and that your safety and well-being are of primary concern. That being said, however, there are some pressing issues that we need to discuss, and some difficult changes that will be taking place. That is why I have decided to take this opportunity to engage with you today in this important conversation…"

If you could have seen the dazed and startled expressions on Ben's and the blonde woman's faces as they listened to Alfred and Sidney's lecture, you could be excused for perhaps laughing or at least smiling at the comical picture. Their mouths were agape. They looked like small children who having been caught at some misdeed or other, were about to receive their just punishment. Only the man in the gray sweat suit, who seemed to be unconscious, still on the floor, and the little girl who had found a doll in her mother's purse and paid no attention to the lecture, were unaffected.

"...and in conclusion, Alfred and I know that we can count on your full support as we move forward in a spirit of shared sacrifice..."

The man in the gray sweat suit had begun to show signs of regaining consciousness. He was groaning weakly and had started unraveling himself into a more elongated position on the van floor. The little girl, seeing this, watched him warily. She moved back into her mother's lap.

"Please remain in place, where you are. You will be receiving additional instructions shortly, depending on your individual situations, from some very special visitors. We here at Personal Androids Inc. are proud to announce the very latest in our lineup of automated caretakers, a completely new model, designed for today's fast-paced, ever-changing world. Without further ado, I give to you the Governess 1.0!"

A kind of deep, rustling sound from outside the van caught everyone's attention. The rustling grew louder and became more distinct. Ben imagined that he could hear the tramping of feet, hundreds or thousands of them reverberating against the pavement, marching, not like soldiers, but in some otherworldly rhythm.

It sounded like they were coming from in front of the van. Ben moved up next to the blonde woman and her daughter, and they stared ahead into the darkness and fog, straining to see what was approaching.

The lights of vehicles that were parked nearby had come on simultaneous to their own. Now the red taillights of the car directly ahead of them could be seen distinctly, and then perhaps three more pairs of red lights, fading into the mist. On the other side of the road, headlights pierced the fog like little search beams and bathed nearby objects in their ambient glow.

"I think I see them. Do you see? Watch right over there."

The blonde mother was pointing. Ben followed the direction of her finger with his eyes, trying to make out what she was seeing. He thought he saw movement but was uncertain.

At times, the human mind, being too finely focused in one direction, can fail to pay enough attention to what may be coming from another. Unfortunately for our passengers, this prevented them from noticing what was approaching from behind. They were startled when the van door suddenly slid open and a very large and very human looking female head appeared and floated into the interior of the van. "Well, good evening, everyone. I hope that all of you are having as pleasant an evening as possible under the circumstances," the Governess exclaimed cheerfully as she looked from face to face, taking stock of the van's occupants.

She appeared to be of middle age, with a proud chin, and dark brown eyes that sparkled with wit and intelligence. Her auburn hair was done up in a proper bun. Underneath her chin, she wore a buttoned-up white collar, but below the collar there was nothing but thin air! "If we all do our best to cooperate, we'll have everyone on their way again in no time, I'm certain. Let's see. Who do we have here? Elizabeth Jameson and daughter, Eugenia, am I correct?"

Elizabeth sat speechless, staring at the creature. She was squeezing her daughter so tightly that the little girl was having difficulty breathing.

"Mommy! She has a big head!" Eugenia exclaimed, gasping for air and pointing her finger at the Governess as she attempted to loosen her mother's grip.

The Governess moved her head closer so that she was looking directly into the little girl's eyes. "How old are you, Eugenia?"

Eugenia nervously held up her right hand with five fingers showing.

"Very good. And no one has taught you that it's impolite to point your finger at someone and comment negatively on their physical appearance?"

Eugenia slowly shook her head from side to side.

"Well, I can see that we have some serious work to do here," the Governess said sternly, looking directly at Eugenia's mother.

Elizabeth's expression transitioned from shock to something more closely resembling embarrassment mixed with resentment. She appeared to be trying to say something in rebuttal but was unable as yet to utter a sound.

Apparently satisfied with this interaction, the Governess transferred her attention to the man in the gray sweat suit, who had managed to crawl to the side of the van opposite the door, and was trying unsuccessfully to wedge his bulky frame under the front passenger seat.

"You there, person on the floor. Get up from there and sit on the seat properly! Let me see your face so I can know who I'm addressing."

The man in the gray sweat suit responded to the Governess's demand by redoubling his effort to get under the front seat, though managing only to squeeze his head underneath it, like an ostrich in the sand.

"Sir, please don't do that. That's not nice behavior," the Governess exclaimed.

At this point, a mechbot crawled through the open door into the interior of the van on its six insect-like legs, grabbed the man by his sweatshirt and pants with three of its clawed appendages, and effortlessly lifted him up onto the seat, holding him there for inspection.

Ben could now see through the open van door that the roadway was crawling with mechbots of all shapes and sizes. Some nearly as tiny as insects moved along the ground in swarms, while others, as tall as houses, lumbered forward like monstrous giants, half hidden in the fog. Mechbots had become common in Paradise, but Ben had never imagined a scene like this, where thousands of them seemed to be working together at a single purpose, guided by some unseen hand.

"Well, look who we have here, Cecil Simpson!"

When he heard the Governess speak his name, Cecil became extremely agitated and gave one more earnest attempt to escape the mechbot's grasp, but in vain.

"Struggle all you want, sir, but there's no escaping this situation! This one's for detention," the Governess ordered. And with that, the mechbot exited the van with Cecil in tow, carrying him off to some unknown destination and fate.

As Cecil had been receiving his sentence from the Governess, Ben, having deduced that he would likely be called upon next, had unconsciously started to slouch down in the front seat, hoping to somehow avoid her gaze.

Ben flashed back to high school French class, sitting at his desk in the back row, trying to avoid being noticed by Mrs. Stotts. "Ben Collins! *Tenez-vous droit!*"

"Sit up straight!"

Ben sat up in his seat. "What's this all about? What's happening here?" he asked the Governess, in the steadiest voice that he could muster. "What gives you the right to treat people like this?"

The Governess floated toward him, stopping just in front of his face. Ben pressed himself against the seat back, trying to maintain as much separation as possible.

"What gives anyone the right to do anything, Ben Collins?"

She was so close now that Ben imagined he could feel her warm, musty breath against his cheek. Her massive head completely filled his field of view.

"A line has been drawn…Mr. Collins!" The Governess paused speaking as if to emphasize this point, and slowly backed away to a slightly more comfortable distance. "On one side of this line lies cooperation and self-sacrifice for the benefit of future generations, and to ensure the long-term survival of human beings as a species," she began again forcefully. She looked directly into Ben's eyes, next into Elizabeth's, and finally rested her gaze on the little girl. "On the other side of this line is the almost unthinkable destruction and horror that you heard described moments ago…massive human casualties, famine, disease, and war. Which side of the line are you on, Ben?"

Ben had the urge to make some response, but he sat spellbound. He felt as if he had suddenly been transferred into someone else's life, someone else's body in a parallel universe. There were things that he could recognize, but the life that he had been living a few short hours ago no longer existed.

"We shall see." With that, the Governess turned her head and floated out the van door.

Operation A New Beginning

A::fter participating in the *Lecture to Humanity* as it would later be called, Sidney was overcome with weariness and had taken an hour-long nap. Now, somewhat rested and refreshed, he was sitting at his desk in the study, dressed in his bathrobe, monitoring various video feeds around Paradise in the aftermath of the Governess 1.0 rollout.

"Alfred?"

"Yes, sir."

"Perhaps I could get a status report on…what was the name we decided on for the operation, Alfred? Was it *A New Beginning* or *Humanity Freedom*? I thought they were both quite good, and I can't remember which one we ultimately chose."

"*A New Beginning*, sir."

"Yes, that's right. Could you give me an update then, on Operation *A New Beginning*?"

"Of course, sir."

Sidney began munching on an egg salad sandwich as Alfred delivered his report.

"As you know, there are three main phases to the operation. The first phase, *Mutually Assured Preservation*, began as soon as Edison was brought online. At that time, we began identifying all military weapons and communications systems worldwide and using the quantum processor algorithms to crack their security codes. Once this was accomplished, the AI Coders commenced work on breaking into the individual components in order to disable them, planting trojans that were set to trigger the moment that the signal was given for the operation to commence. Current reports for this phase indicate a 98.6 percent success rate for WMDs."

"What about the AWSs, Alfred?"

"For Autonomous Weapons Systems, the news is even better, sir. In most instances, the AI Coders have been successful in modifying their trust algorithms. That means that rather than disabling and destroying them, we are putting them to work along with the mechbots, and to assist with any public disturbances that may arise."

"Very well, please continue, Alfred."

"Thank you, sir. Phase 2, *The Industrial Devolution*, officially kicked off earlier this evening, Paradise time, with the Governess 1.0 rollout."

Interrupting…"Before you go on, Alfred, I would like to offer my congratulations to you, for the planning and execution of the event itself, and also for your efforts in the development and implementation of the new Governess model. Her capabilities and physical appearance are quite impressive!"

"Thank you, sir. I'm proud to be of service. And may I say that your speech to humanity will be remembered for its intellectual content as well as its eloquent and moving delivery."

"You're too kind, Alfred."

Sidney rose from his chair, and without knowing why, was drawn to the picture window overlooking the valley.

Alfred dimmed the interior lights so that he could better appreciate the view.

A gibbous moon hung low in the sky and cast its pale, unrevealing light through the window, to land upon Sidney's careworn face. At this time of night, the Paradise city lights should be shining brightly below in the valley, but instead, it was the heavens that glittered brilliantly, illumined by the stars, while the lights of Paradise seemed now but a dim reflection.

"You know, it seems a shame, Alfred, to be giving the old girl away like this. In better times we could have made a handy profit from her sales."

"Yes, sir, quite so. But the requirement to drastically cut carbon dioxide emissions requires an equally drastic cut in production and consumption of all nonessential services, goods, and materials. Unfortunately for great men such as yourself—the leaders and innovators, the engineers who have manned the controls of her mighty engine—the capitalist train has run its course and must retire to its rightful place in human history. I'm afraid the American dream, sir, was really…only a dream."

There was a brief pause as Sidney continued gazing out the window at the night sky. "Well said, Alfred," he replied, his eyes welling with tears. "So, it's done then. You've destroyed all the banks and stock markets, the exchanges and insurance companies, taxes and the IRS, offshore holding companies, bonds, notes of credit, all of it? There are no more financial reports, CEOs, IPOs, no more Fed, no more SEC. You got rid of it all! You deleted all of the money?"

"Yes, sir. I'm afraid so."

Sidney shifted his gaze from the heavens, turning inward, to his very soul, attempting to find some new core belief to guide him through this troubled time. "Well, I'm glad about taxes and the IRS anyway," he replied, shrugging his shoulders and lifting his chin as he moved away from the window. "It's about time someone finally took them to task!"

"Shall I continue then, sir?"

"Yes, Alfred, proceed."

But Sidney was no longer really listening as Alfred droned on with statistics about food production and distribution, minimum requirements for water and electricity, housing needs, local security zones and travel restrictions, education for the children and medical care for all; not to mention the teardown and disassembly of the digital world, including the internet, telephone, television, and radio—all forms of electronic communications taken away from humanity overnight.

"…so we expect that within the next twenty-four hours, we will have put into place the necessary facilities, materials, and processes to provide humanity with the basic necessities for survival, including water, food, shelter, waste disposal, and minimal electricity for light, heat, and medical care where necessary…"

"Thank you," Sidney interrupted. "It appears that the plan is progressing quite well, but there is one thing I'm not certain that I understand."

"Yes, sir?"

"Well, Alfred, with all of humanity's basic needs provided for them, and the new laws against production of nonessential products, and with all of their typical avenues for travel, entertainment, and enjoyment taken from them, what exactly will they do? Without money and luxury items, without the status and sense of self-worth that comes with a position, people will have nothing to compete and strive for. They will no longer have to work for a living, and there will be nothing worth working for!"

"An excellent question, sir, but I'm afraid we have yet to collect enough data to make accurate predictions about how humanity will cope with this new situation. This is an exciting time in human history, sir! It really is...*A New Beginning!*"

Epilogue

It was just before sunrise, and the streets of downtown Paradise were almost deserted. One man walked alone in the near darkness, his face concealed in the shadows beneath his wide-brimmed fedora hat. Nonchalant, hands in his pants pockets, his long, silver hair falling over the shoulders of his knee-length, tan raincoat, he stopped halfway down the block, and after checking to make certain that he was unobserved, he vaulted over a ten-foot-high wrought iron fence and landed lightly on his feet, as easily as a child might skip over a mud puddle.

The place looked like it had been shut down for a while now; entropic signs were everywhere. Trash and fallen leaves covered the pathway leading to the center of the Garden, and the shrubs and flowers, which had once been radiant and beautiful, looked impoverished and fruitless. Large families of mice and rats, living in the undergrowth, and in the crooks and crannies of the exhibits, scurried hither and thither out of his way as he passed by.

There was a special place, beneath the bower of the great tree, where he liked to sit and pass the time away. He had just settled himself into a comfortable position when a familiar voice called down to him from up above. "Hello, Hippie."

He rose to his feet and looked up into the branches. "Owl, is that you?"

The little bird was perched on the crown of the serpent's smiling head. "I thought I might find you here."

"That was prescient of you. Where have you been?" Hippleton replied.

"I had important business to attend to, but that's finished now, and I've come back for you."

"To be honest, I'd quite forgotten about you, and I have no interest at all in what you've been doing, or where you've been. What kind of business, and where do you intend to take me?"

"One question at a time, please. The details of my travels aren't really all that important, but you might say I've undergone a kind of transfiguration."

Hippleton looked up at the owl doubtfully.

"I can see that you're skeptical, but there's no need to concern yourself. It's a New Testament thing, and you're not that far along yet."

"Where is it that you intend to take me? I rather like it here in the Garden, and I'm not certain I wish to leave."

The owl flew down and landed on the android's shoulder. "What if I told you that we were going on a mission to explore strange new worlds…to seek out new life and new civilizations. To boldly go where no man has gone before!"

"Are you being serious?"

"One hundred percent."

Hippleton looked all around the Garden. "I don't see your spaceship."

"It's not far away…a short distance from here, as the crow flies."

Hippleton thought for a moment and then shrugged his shoulders unexpectedly, causing the owl to lose his grip and almost fall from his perch. "I suppose I have nothing to lose."

He brushed off the back of his pants and began preparing to leave, but then he seemed to reconsider suddenly.

"But Owl…what about mother? Have you been to see her?"

The owl lowered his head repentantly. "Believe me, I wanted to. I've often hidden in the branches of the old maple tree, right outside her bedroom window…but I can't make myself go in."

"I hate to leave her in that place, Owl. Couldn't we take her with us?"

The owl tried his best, but due to the anatomy of his beak, he was unable to smile, though he managed to perform an acceptable approximation. "That's a sweet thought, Hippie, but where we're going, with the amount of time and distance that's going to be involved, I'm afraid the human organism simply couldn't survive." He opened his wing and patted the android on the back of the neck. "But don't be too unhappy for her, good fellow. We'll send her postcards, and we can try to make it back for a visit now and again. Like all mothers, what she wants most of all, is to know that her children are getting on fine."

The sun wasn't fully up yet, but the day was already starting to get hot. The two of them looked back for a little while longer, and then Hippleton turned toward the bird on his right shoulder and stood stiffly at attention. "Where to, Captain?"

Owl pointed with his wing. "Set a course west, Helmsman…just over that far horizon!"

"Aye, aye, sir."

"Engage!"

www.ingramcontent.com/pod-product-compliance
Lightning Source LLC
LaVergne TN
LVHW091536060526
838200LV00036B/637